MISTRESS B-0003

GARDEN OF THE GODS

A. A. DARK

Mad Girl
PUBLISHING
PITCH BLACK™

Mistress B-0003
Garden of the Gods
International Bestselling Author
A.A. Dark
Copyright © 2022 by A.A.Dark

All Rights Reserved

AUTHOR'S NOTE

Garden of the Gods is a collection of standalone novellas shadowing the lives of the Mistresses and Masters who occupy it. Although each main character will only have ONE book, they may appear in others throughout the series. Some stories will also have BDSM elements, but these stories are NOT BDSM. Mistress and Master is a title, showing nothing more than owner-ship. The scale of darkness in the stories will range from Pitch Black, Static White, to the extreme, Oblivion. Please be aware of this before you dive in. The rating will be in the blurb of each book. Trigger warnings are all over the board. If you are not comfortable with dark reads, please DO NOT read this series.

RULES

GARDEN OF THE GODS

Rules are subject to change. If you neglect to follow these rules, you will undergo an investigation/trial where punishment is evaluated by the Board and Main Master, Elec Wexler. Punishment can range from fines to lockup in Hell Row to Death.

1) Keep your hands to yourself.

2) The only property you may destroy is your own. (slaves included.)

3) You are a number. Your peers are a number. Use them.

4) Respect your neighbor's privacy.

5) GOTG is NOT to be discussed outside of this facility.

GLOSSARY

W

Virgin slave. Wears a white robe during the auction.

B

Nonvirgin slave. Wears a blue robe during the auction.

D

Docile, drugged slave. Can be W or B. Heavily trained. Good for elderly or those with disabilities.

M

Male slave.

Crow

Ruined, disfigure slave. Convicts fall into this category. Women or men that fall into the breeding category. Black robe during the auction. The cheapest slaves.

Blank slate

Mostly male slaves who have undergone forced indoctrination through various scientific methods. (Brainwashing, programming, training, etc.) They're programmed to be focused solely on their Mistress or Master. They are made to be obedient, loyal, and protective.

"TIME HAS NO RESPECT FOR BEAUTY."

ERZEBET BATHORY, THE COUNTESS 2009

PROLOGUE

Garden of the Gods
Colorado Springs Underground Facility

"This is the beta run. Even though you have taken classes, and even though our slaves have been trained, no position as Master or Mistress is set in stone until you can prove you're worthy of the title. So far, you've passed enough tests to make it here to our first auction, but who are you? I'll tell you. You are the wealthy. The powerful. Influential. That got you here, but that's where it ends. Inside the Gardens, you have no name; you have a number. Your identity or status in the outside world means absolutely nothing. Zero. Here, there is no power or favoritism. This is my world, and you are no one. Let that sink in." He paused, staring us all down. "You are no one. The only thing that connects all of you is ...*you're all fucking sick.*"

Laughter echoed in the large theater-type setting. Everything from the crème-colored silk chairs we all sat in, to the pale lavender velvet accents, invoked welcome. Just as the Main Master, Elec Wexler did through his introduction as he continued.

"Tonight is the first night of endless more auctions. A small majority of you come to us from Whitlock[1]. Take note, this is not that place. The rules are different. The location is different. Do not mistake me for your old Main Master. I am not Bram Whitlock. The Garden of the Gods will never fall."

Silence.

"For those who are new, let me explain how this works. We start the bidding with the white, or w's [2]for short. These are the virgins. From there, we move to the b's: or blue[3]." He paused, raising one of his eyebrows sarcastically. "*You guessed it*: not virgins. The d's[4] will follow. They're docile, trained, and good for those who are looking for a long-term slave. Lastly, come the black, or as we call them, the crows[5]. They're not your typical slave. These are the cheap, buy-one-get-one-half-off sort of deals. They are the convicts. The disfigured. The breeders. Some are plain repulsive." He shrugged. "And if you're into it, old. You get it. Like I said, not typical for a place where beauty and sterilization are usually the standard."

"For the Mistresses or those looking for our programmable, 'blank slate' [6]males, your auction is just through that door off to the right. The information was in your packet, but just in case you missed it, these are the males who have had portions of their memories erased. They know who they are, but they only remember what we want them to. We'd like to think when it comes to security issues, we've learned from the past. Like I said before, we're in the beta stages, but we're assured these male slaves are safe. Since we're doing our own trial run, you can get them at a steal. They will take orders. They will obey no matter what the demand is. Use your imagination. If you're still having trouble understanding, read more about each of these in the pamphlet."

He turned, pointing, but continued. "Some of you are here to spill blood. Some want sex beyond the norm. Here, there are no

2

rules. What you buy is yours. Do with it what you will. Fuck it. Kill it. Eat it."

Elec walked down the length of the stage. He wore a black fitted suit with a matching black button-up shirt and tie. His dark hair was on the shorter side, and his handsome features couldn't be overlooked. From anyone in the large audience, they'd see he addressed the crowd in comfort. He wasn't afraid of public speaking—he thrived in his new position. His tall length stood straight, yet he walked with ease as his light eyes took in everything. For those who knew or remembered Bram Whitlock[7], there was no mistaking the resemblance. Elec's father was siblings with Bram's mother. Both boys' genes ran deep on the Wexler side.

"If you look down the arm of the chair, you will see a button. Do not." He stopped, turning in a slow circle to view everyone in the room. "Let me say it again, so I'm not accused of not making myself clear. *Do not*...press that button unless you are sure you want to bid. Also...do not continue bidding if you don't have the money. Here, there's no such thing as accidents. If you bid, you buy. If you can't pay, I will take my payment however I see fit. Your business. Your house. Your hand." His eyes narrowed. "*Your life.* I am not your friend. I am not going to take it easy on you. If you cross me, you're dead. If you lie to me, I will cut out your tongue, and then you will die. Honesty is everything. Remember that."

"The rules are easy, but acceptance into the Garden of the Gods comes at a price. You signed a contract to get this far. You know the 'dos and don'ts'. Memorize them. It could mean your life if you forget."

Lights raced the length of the circumference, illuminating the edge of the floor, and running over the top arches of multiple doorways. Gasps and chatter filled the theater and heads spun from the stage to the nearest entrance as a line of the most beautiful women adorned in sheer, white robes awaited their cue.

"Now that we got that out of the way; prepare to empty your wallets. This is the fun part. You're about to have your wildest, bloodiest dreams come true. Happy bidding, Masters and Mistresses. I have no doubts you'll enjoy."

MISTRESS B-0003

F or an underground military installation, Garden of the Gods was exactly as I expected. At least, at first. The electronic doors to get in were heavily guarded. My every move had been watched: physically and digitally. I was escorted by two guards at all times as they weaved me through dull, cement halls. Eventually, we took an elevator down for what felt like forever. Once it opened, more halls until…something inside me sparked. A large gate appeared, giving view to a dream. One I'd had for so long, I could *feel* myself come to life. It was real emotion: excitement. Not pretend, like my occupation as an actress made me mimic. Delight. Anticipation. They blossomed inside me promising a truth I wouldn't have to hide anymore.

The double, golden doors that greeted me were thick. Large snakes rested in the middle of each door, and symbols were engraved down every inch around them. The gate had to have been almost twenty feet tall and stood opened. The sight alone had me slowing as I approached. What I saw as I headed through the main entrance was another world altogether.

Apple trees. They led to the cornucopia of amenities and shops that made up the main street for the city. On each side of the fifteen-foot path rested everything from restaurants to boutiques. Even salons and clubs of every kind were fitted in-between as I peered down to the empty and intersecting roads. It was as if I were in a ghost city, and it was waiting for its residents to come to life for its grand opening.

Something flickered above and pulled my eyes from the flashing signs that welcome me forward. Up and up my stare traveled, trying to make sense of what I was seeing.

"Is that?"

I didn't have the words to continue. The building was painted just as black as the void above, disappearing into the darkness. There appeared to be so many levels, I couldn't tell how many floors there were as I looked up. If it wasn't for the random lights coming on from apartments above, I wouldn't have even noticed the building completely surrounding the circular city at all.

"This way, Mistress."

The disorienting maze hadn't ended with my new home. As I followed the guards inside, I quickly learned things weren't quite what they seemed. The outdoor city was a speck of what made up the Garden of the Gods. More cameras. More uniformed guards at every turn as we weaved inside another type of indoor city. When we got in a glass elevator, I really got a dose of what our new world was about, and some floors catered more for the depraved. Toy shops. Weapons. Animals. From stables to armories, to a grocery floor, to a hospital wing I couldn't see inside of, there seemed to be nothing this place didn't have.

It took roughly fifteen minutes, but I finally was led to an apartment on the fourteenth floor. An apartment I styled months ago, but I was never given the information on where it was located. My smile was automatic the moment I saw my creation, and it hadn't left me in the hours since. It stayed in place even now as I ran my hands down my black silk dress. My day at the salon had been nothing compared to what I'd undergone for the

Oscars, but I looked phenomenal. After all, this was the beginning of something great, something I'd waited my entire life for, and if I was taught anything, it was to go into the unknown looking your best.

"Mistresses, I know some of you were not happy to hear you'd been separated from the main auction, but this is a necessity for those of you who seek out males. You've taken your classes. Those of you who are interested in the blank slates know the risks and what to expect. Trust me when I say it is safer this way. Now, if you'll follow me, we can get your own auction started."

Elec, the Main Master, had us gathered off to the side of the auditorium that was in full swing with bids. The room we walked through was dark, haloed with blue lights that lit up morbid paintings of gold and silver. Arched, closed doors filled the wide hallway, and white light flooded the space as he headed deeper into the building, gesturing to multiple leather sofas adorned with large binders. His eyes scanned the crowd as women gathered in from behind.

"This is your auction room. There are two of you to each sofa. Pictures of male slaves fill those binders. The ones that are blank slates or programmable are marked with the blue star. If you see one you like, you're to head to that machine over there and enter the information. A guard will escort you to the slave's cell. There, he will be restrained. You can go in and do what you must, but a warning," he said sternly. "If you kill, maim, or put so much as a scratch on my slave, you will buy him at a price I deem fit. If you can't afford that price, I will find a way to get my money out of you. Do you understand?"

I nodded, hearing mummers behind me.

"If you find a slave you wish to purchase, you return to your seat and enter your choice into the system. There are forty-four of you. There are over five hundred males. The auction will be first-come, first-served. Just because you chose one does not

7

exclude others from changing their minds from their own choice and bidding on your slave. After you've won your slave, the code word you chose in your application will be programmed to your property. Delivery is immediate. Any issues that arise will be taken care of with that one word. This applies to all slaves, not just the blank slates. Without going into too much detail, we have paired with secret government sources and made it our priority that whether you're female, old, weak, you are *always* safe. This code word will immobilize on recognition, so...don't say your code word unless you mean to disable your slave. If for some reason you need assistance outside of that, we have guards on the opposite end of every floor. Their number is pound zero-zero. They will arrive at your location immediately. Any questions?"

"Yes." I cleared my throat, staying in my role. *Cold. Confident.* "What if I wish to buy both male and female?"

"Both?"

One of Elec's brows raised, only for him to shrug. "The w's[1] are already going fast. If a virgin is what you're after, I suggest you not waste time. Find me in the main auction room when you're ready. It's right back through the door. Anything else?"

"No."

"Great," he said, readdressing the crowd. "You'll find your Mistress number assigned to the table next to your seat. Happy bidding."

As fast as he'd come, Main Master Elec departed. I was sure he had to return to the other auction, but I wasn't a fan of how us women were separated. I didn't dwell on it as I headed forward, searching for my number. I was Beta-Mistress Three. Beta, but not for long. I had no intention of not having this work out. I'd prove I was worthy, and I'd be an Alpha. I'd be a real Mistress, and I'd disappear from the outside world forever if I chose to. It didn't suit me anyway. I was made for this. Made and born for the darker side of this world.

M0088

Male eighty-eight. I had to have read the title on the inside of my door a million and one times in the last eleven months. Had it been that long? I hadn't known until my medical appointment only hours ago. Eleven months. It felt like a fucking eternity after all I'd been through. As if I'd been in a dream that lasted an entire lifetime. A dream I prayed was coming to an end.

Aside from the constant training videos, human interaction was few and far between. A grab from a guard on shower day. A hold to the bicep as a nurse shot me up with lord only knew what. They didn't talk to us just for conversation. They wouldn't even look us in the eyes when they were giving their lessons. I wasn't sure how many times I thought I'd break or scream until I really lost it. The psychotic episodes were endless, but perhaps they did what they meant to. I was up for auction, and I could be sold. Or…I would be if I were chosen, and although I faced certain death, I could have cried for the relief that gave me. A relief that could have gone both ways. As confusing as it was, I wanted anything other than this. Even if it was the worst thing imaginable. I didn't care. I prayed I was picked. I prayed for a miracle upon miracles to end this torture.

Even the dimmed light gave me hope. If it was day it was bright, but at night it was pitch black. This was nice. New. A year ago, I wouldn't have gotten excited over a fucking light. I had it made. I was in my second year of Yale. I was there on a full ride, and I just knew I was going to become someone far exceeding my piece of shit stepdad and absent real father. I was going to make it and take care of my mom the way she should have been doted on, but then I went to a stupid house-party. I never attended those things. I much preferred to go to a legitimate establishment, but this one was different. It was a mile down the road in a house I prayed someday to afford. I mainly went to check the place out and dream of my future, but I grabbed a beer, despite that I wasn't old enough.

Nothing.

I couldn't have drunk a quarter of that beer before all color faded and I passed out. When I awoke, I was strapped down to a bed. That only lasted for a day when I was moved to the underground trafficking system. I couldn't believe it at first. It was a network of subterranean highways. I even got to see how it housed little cubbies off to the side on one of my bathroom breaks. Inside, there was a bed, toilet, and shower. It was a mini hotel room, and outside of some of them I even witnessed multiple vending machines. I shouldn't have seen all that, but from where I was kept so close to the front, I was tall enough to peer over the glass. It was scary, but the hell didn't start until I got here. Then, the nightmare of being processed and detained happened, breaking me down even more.

I barely remembered any of that now…

My eyes left my slave number posted on the door and lowered to my nude, muscled frame. If I did anything, it was workout. It was all I could do to pass the time and try to keep sane. I couldn't help now but wonder if it would pay off. It hadn't even dawned on me before but…more hope? I'd been undressed like this for an hour. Would the auction last all night? How would I know it was over?

My mind said it didn't matter, even though I felt deep down it did. I tried holding to the concerns pouring through despite an internal voice telling me not to worry about those either. The voice was always there, always telling me what to think or how to feel.

Curiosity returned and with it, the ache as I stared around the room. I couldn't stay here another night. Not one more. Not one. If I didn't get chosen, how long before the next auction? Were they weekly? Monthly? What if no one ever picked me? What if I spent another ten years rotting away in this cell all because I didn't look as good as I did from when they'd taken me? And looks definitely had something to do with it. Every slave I'd come into contact with in the last year had been gorgeous. I wasn't naïve that women thought I was attractive. Hell, I was barraged at college, despite alienating myself to focus on my studies. Maybe that was isolated. To these buyers, I could very well not be good enough.

A strangled sound left me as I shifted and pulled the few inches I was allowed from the chains. Buzzing caused me to jump, and my breath hitched as my door electronically opened. A guard surged in, meeting my eyes dead-on. The shock and intensity had me immediately lowering mine. Despite that I was sure I could protect myself outside of these chains, I'd been beaten and trained enough to know what not to do. I couldn't ruin any chance I had of getting out of this room now.

My stare shot to my feet as the guard tugged at the restraints on my wrists and checked the ones at my ankles. When he lifted, I braved a glance up. He had his back to me and was nodding at someone outside. Even though I knew I'd get in trouble if I were caught, my head tried to move over, but I couldn't see around the man's wide frame. *Guilt. The voice.* I shouldn't have done that. I had to obey everything I was taught. I had to follow orders.

"He's secure. You may enter."

"He's a blank slate[1]? You're sure?"

"Yes, Mistress. He's very aware. He'll even appear semi-normal, but his focus will be primarily on you. With what he's undergone, he won't be able to help it. You will be safe."

"That's what they keep telling me. Let's find out."

He walked out and any thought or breath I may have held vanished just as fast. I was dead. There was no other way to make sense of what I was seeing. It simply wasn't real. It couldn't be. Not even in my wildest dreams would I have ever come face to face with the movie star, Charlotte Wyce. She was beyond famous. Maybe the most recognized and important female celebrity to exist. She was an activist for women's rights. She was *the* voice for domestic violence. How many movies had I watched and drooled over her? And she was here, walking right in my direction in the sexiest silk dress I'd ever seen? No. She was a vision or hallucination. What I was seeing couldn't be real.

"This is surprising. You're better than the pictures," she breathed out, staring up and down my body. "Your brown hair is shorter now. In your profile, it reached down to your cheeks." Her head tilted as she studied me. "Strong jaw. Nice lips. Light green eyes. Very light." She got closer in the dimness, narrowing her lids. "Unbelievable. You would have had such potential in Hollywood. I think I like you so far." When her stare stayed on mine, I forced a swallow, immediately lowering my gaze. I couldn't think. It was impossible to form any sort of rational thought. How was any of this logical? I was a slave. Disposable if my owner deemed it so. That's what I was taught. The Main Master said, expect to be beaten, cut up…killed. You won't make it out of here alive. *He'd said that during the tour.* It's what I had been told for months. Was it true? It had to be but…why her? How could she do something like that?

The voice returned telling me not to even think about it. That wasn't my concern, she was. Just her.

"I said I liked you; what do you think of me, slave? Do you know who I am?"

My eyes rose at her question as I tried to get my thoughts in order. It had been so long since I actually communicated with someone. The huskiness of her voice had the ultimate lure, screwing me up even more. I'd seen Charlotte act seductive. I knew exactly how her expression appeared when lust took over. Her lips grew poutier, and her lids lowered just the smallest amount. *Just as they were now as she moved in even closer to me.* Fuck, for the life of me I couldn't breathe, more or less think. But I had to. Somehow I knew my life depended on it.

"I know who you are...Mistress."

"Mmm." She moaned the smallest amount, closing her eyes and smiling. "I like the way you say that. Say it again."

"Mistress."

Fingers ran over my stomach, dipping between my defined abs as she went even lower. A sound left me, and I knew I was rock hard as I stiffened. That touch...and coming from Charlotte Wyce of all people. It was like an explosion to any common sense I might have had left. And her perfume: it reminded me of a soap I'd been gifted once from my roommate's girlfriend. Cherry almond but with extra spice. It was so foreign to smell anything outside of food. It was an assault to my senses, but in an intoxicating way. It opened cravings I hadn't felt in forever. Needs. Wants. How I managed to force out my question, I wasn't sure.

"If you buy me, do you plan to kill me?"

Teeth bit into her lip and she straightened. "I hope not. That will be entirely up to you." She looked over her shoulder towards the guard. "Privacy."

Only seconds went by before the sound of mechanics filled the space and the door closed. Big blue eyes met mine, and for the life of me, I couldn't break my stare and be the slave I needed to be. She was back to making a path with her fingers over my stomach, lowering enough to trace the length of my cock with her fingertip.

"I was encouraged by other Mistresses outside to use you how I want. As if fucking you right here would make all the difference in my choice. It won't. What I'm looking for from you is a lot more, but I do want to test you out, slave. I'm going to ask you a list of questions. You're going to be honest with me or I move to my next choice. I don't have much time, and I won't waste it on someone who's not a good fit. Do you understand?"

My heart slammed hard in my chest. *Hope. Hope. Hope.* It hammered into me with every beat overriding the voice that almost never left. No death…just her and whatever she needed me to do…if I passed her test.

"Yes, Mistress."

She gripped around my cock, swirling over my head to collect the pre-cum so she could stroke smoothly down my thick length.

"Do you like women, slave? Sexually?"

"Yes."

"What about me? Do you find me attractive?"

My eyes widened in disbelief. She was Charlotte fucking Wyce. Who hadn't jacked off to her movies or pics online? I sure as hell had, countless times, even if she was a good ten-to-fifteen years older than me. Couldn't she see my cock? Feel it? Fuck, I didn't want her to stop. My training would have encouraged this as good behavior.

"I do. I." Words disappeared as she slightly increased the speed.

"What is your favorite movie of mine?"

Thinking was beyond me as I closed my eyes. The pleasure was too much. The sensations were like a wave of euphoria I never wanted to leave. Instinct was all I had.

"Beneath the Fire. Hands down." I moaned, trying to continue. "It was the only movie I really saw you embrace. You were unbelievable in the others, but that one…that one you shined in. You liked your character. You were her."

Her hand stopped, and my throat nearly closed as I opened my eyes and met her hard stare.

"Impressive." She glanced to the door a bit confused or surprised, but she turned back to gazing into my face. "You see through me more than most. I'm not sure if that's good or bad." Hesitation. "That movie wasn't very popular."

"It should have been. You were a goddess in that film despite the hardships your character faced. You lived them with her. I think even a part of you died at the end with her as well."

"A goddess…I like that. You may be right." Her hand squeezed but loosened and began stroking again. "You're more normal than I thought you would be. Or…more aware. I need a slave I have chemistry with. One who can read me. Who can get into a routine and make me happy. A slave who sees me. *Only me*. How loyal are you?"

Death, this room, or property of Charlotte Wyce? Was it even debatable? She didn't need a slave if all she was looking for was an obsessive companion. She could have had her choice on the outside world for free. Even in my muddled, broken state, I knew something wasn't right. There was a catch some-where, but did I care if it got me out of here alive…*with her*? *Her. Her.*

My shoulders squared, mirroring my internal thoughts, and maybe she picked up on it as well. "You won't find anyone more loyal. Or in awe," I said under my breath. "I would be lucky but honored."

Saying the words and knowing they were the truth, a part of me felt lighter. It felt right. With my admission out loud, it was as if I handed myself over to her completely.

"Honored. You're good with words, but I'll expect you to

prove that loyalty to me over and over in more ways than you can imagine. Let's start right now," she purred.

She pulled the dress to rest at her hips, lowering her matching panties high on her thighs so my cock could rest just inside the silk. I couldn't tear my gaze from her smooth pussy as she rubbed it against me. The stroking increased while she teased the head over her clit. Her free hand grabbed my shoulder, gripping tightly as she took me back deeper towards her entrance. My fists clenched and sweat covered my body as the ecstasy became overwhelming. Right now, she wanted loyalty in the form of my cum, plain and simple, and I sure as fuck wasn't going to deny her. I couldn't on so many levels it made my head spin.

"Prove yourself to me, slave." She moaned. "Give me your honor. Your loyalty. Show me how much you want to be mine."

She was so wet and hot as she stroked me faster against her. A part of me far back in the distance knew this was wrong. The nagging even tried to break through the lust, but I pushed it so far away, I prayed it'd never return. A good minute or two went by as my hips rocked with her strokes. I could hear both of our sounds growing. I was right there, being triggered as her juices soaked me. More time as the caressing and whimpers warped my mind even more. *Me. Her. Me. Her. Together. As hers. Loyal.*

"Fuck. Fuck, Mistress. I. Fuck." My cock thickened as she reached up and pulled against the back of my neck, bringing my mouth to hers. On contact, cum shot so hard from me, my knees almost gave out. I didn't even remember what it was like to have an orgasm, but here, now, I never wanted to forget. For the first time in almost a year…blinding hope soared through. Real hope. And emotions. They engulfed me, dragging me into a thick fog as the voice spoke a mantra in my mind. *With her. For her. Her. Us.*

"Yes. Yes." Whimpers followed her spasms as she jolted from the sensitivity. I was still rolling the waves of my orgasm, and Charlotte's panties were already filled with my cum, just as I suspected she'd planned.

"Mistress, buy me." My forehead lowered to hers as her body sagged into mine. It was forbidden for me to ask anything of her, but I couldn't help myself or shake the feeling as if we were meant to be together. As if...I belonged to her. I did, didn't I? The voice claimed I did. The voice said I was hers, and it couldn't be wrong. Panic. It hit hard at the thought of us not being together after this. "I'll do anything you want. *I'll worship you.* Protect you. You can have every part of me. Anything, Mistress. I'm yours completely."

"Anything?" She pulled up her panties, keeping a part of me with her. *My cum.* At the realization, my heart stopped completely. Me...*with her.* Me, meaning enough to her to keep on her most private part? That had to mean she wanted me. There was potential with me as her slave. There was...an us. An actual life of some form. With her. "Focus, slave. Last questions, and these are the hardest." *Charlotte Wyce. Mine? Hers?* She bit her lip, pressing her digits into her soaked panties as she moaned, befuddling my mind again. It was her lowering her dress that snapped me back to reality. "Do you think you could ever love me?"

Didn't the tiniest piece of me already? Something was there.

"I'd love you more than anyone."

"Would you fight for me?"

Anger, an emotion that had been stripped of me months ago, roared to life at her words. Fight. I could do that too, couldn't I? I sure felt like a fighter. Hadn't my stepdad owned a training gym? Why couldn't I remember?

"Take me to them."

"Would you bleed for me?"

"Whenever you want."

"Great, but not good enough. Would you kill for me?"

Pausing, I studied her serious stare. There it was. Death. It wasn't coming for me, but it was coming, and I was going to be the one calling it in. Could I do that? For her? *Her. Her.* Like a robot, I couldn't tear my stare from her beautiful face as I listened to the voice brand her even more into my mind. *Her. Us.*

"If killing is what you want, I'll make it the most gruesome death there's ever been."

A smile, one that I felt myself softening towards. Love, yes. Us. No more room. No more alone.

"Good, slave. Maybe you'll be able to prove yourself soon enough."

WO166

"She means nothing to me. I want her, but not yet. I need to bond with my other slave first. I don't want to have to worry about both at the same time."

"Mistress." The Main Master's voice hardened as he looked between me and the woman I assumed had bought me. Had I been relieved after seeing all the old, nasty men who'd surrounded and touched me on my way to the stage? I wasn't so sure I should be anymore. This gorgeous, older woman was cold. Cruel even as she glared towards me. "If you weren't ready for two slaves, you shouldn't have bought them both at the same time."

"I have plans for her, just not yet. I need her to stay…" she flicked her hand to the side as if I were garbage, "wherever she was before. I mean, does my money mean nothing? It should at least pay for room and board. All I need is a week. Two, tops. Maybe not even that long."

"This isn't a hotel, Mistress Three."

"But I need the time."

"To bond with your male slave?"

The woman raised one of her eyebrows, and I couldn't shake

how I knew her from somewhere. She was so beautiful and completely my opposite. Where she had dark hair, I had pale blonde. She was tall; I was short. She had a dream body, and I was pole-straight with barely any breasts or hips.

"To bond. *To test*. To do whatever the fuck I want. You said it yourself at the auction: fuck them, kill them, eat them, or something of that nature."

"I did."

"So let me and keep your judgment to yourself. Just keep this slave for the time being for me, *please*. I'll get her out of your hair soon enough."

"No. You have to take her now. Shackles are standard in every room, and you have your code word if you need it. You'll be fine."

"For fuck's sake. I know I'll be fine. I'm not worried about my safety; I just don't want to see her face." Again, a glare. One filled with such hate and anger, it had me stepping back.

I wasn't going to cry again. I wouldn't do it. Yet, the tears were already escaping me. In the seven months since I'd been here, they hadn't stopped. I'd never get used to this or forget how perfect my life had been.

Okay, maybe not perfect. Maybe not even close. Compared to this, though, it was easy. How had I thought the worst thing in the world was not fitting in? Friends didn't define who I was. Being head cheerleader at my old high school didn't do that. After going from the most popular girl to no one, I'd been so depressed, making a fool of myself to fit into my new town. All for what? For no one to want to hang out with me because they were already established in their own little groups? Who cared! It wasn't a slave cell I had to live in. It wasn't complete isolation away from everyone like now. I'd still had my parents. My sisters. *Freedom*. What did I have now? Nothing but death to look forward to. The Main Master had said so.

"Weak. Pathetic. Do you see why I can't keep her yet? This is not even a slave, it's a weakling."

"Tough. You bought her. You're going to take her with you or just kill her right here and now. I don't have time, Mistress. I have other matters to attend to. Is there anything else you need? An escort back to your apartment, perhaps?"

"I do, but not for me; for this thing," she snapped. "Let them take her. I have to go collect my real slave."

"He's already been delivered and restrained in your apartment. We took care of that for you since you did the double auction. You're free to take this one and go." The Main Master's eyes flickered to me, but he held the same expression she had: distaste.

"Great. Fine. Let's go, *weakling*." Stilettos clicked against the floor as she took off at a fast pace. "If you so much as try to run, I'll immobilize you and spill your blood right on these hideous cement floors. You'd be smart to keep your mouth shut and hide from me as much as you can. Your life literally depends on it."

The dark-haired woman kept talking as she stormed ahead. The fact that I still wore the sheer white robe should have made me feel insecure, but I was over anything but the fear of the woman's words. She was going to kill me. Maybe not right now, but soon. Today. Tomorrow. I was going to die, and one wrong move on my part would seal my fate.

Sniffling, I tried to stop the sob that wanted to come. The sound had me almost colliding with her as she spun and got an inch from my face. Shaking was taking over her body and her eyes were abnormally round with pure evil. She was beyond angry. She was livid and no doubt wondering if I was even worth going another step for. I collapsed to my knees, trembling as I stared ahead blankly. Isn't that what our training taught us to do? Kneel to heal. Kneel...or be killed.

"Stand up. *You're a woman.* How are you so weak?"

21

I obeyed, rising back to my feet. As I took in her words, I tried to understand where they came from, but I couldn't. Weak? I was scared. She meant to kill me. I was taken from my family. Poked, prodded, sterilized. Was I not allowed to show emotion at the crescendo of my fate? Everything had led up to this exact moment, and I couldn't numb myself enough to hide it.

"I better not hear another sound out of you. Not one."

She left me there, the clicking of her heels against the cold cement floor had me racing to catch up. Snot ran down my lips while I wiped it away. True to her order, I refused to sniffle again. The tears still came, but I didn't mimic the heartbreak. I got on the elevator, keeping my head lowered. Being invisible, just like she wanted. Maybe if I were stronger, I would have run and invited certain death, but she was right. I was too weak for that. I didn't want to die. Not yet. After whatever this woman had planned, I might come to regret that.

The elevator opened and a voice stopped my new Mistress in her tracks as she began to exit. "You're...No way. I'll be damned. You're that actress. The one who played Kitty Swanson in that one flick. Charlotte. What's the last name. One minute, it's right there. Charlotte—"

"Did you not read the rules? We don't go by names here. I'm sorry, *who are you*?"

The sourness in my Mistress's tone was back at the man's gawking. My stare shot up to the older woman. She had to be in her mid-thirties despite she really didn't look like it. Me, I appeared every day of my measly seventeen years. But an actress? Is that why she felt so familiar? Had I seen her before?

"I'm Master seventy-one. I'm Norman Free. I was at Whit-lock before it went to shit."

"That tells me nothing. You know who I am. *Who* are you?"

We finally left the elevator to come to stand next to a balding man in his fifties. He had a slight wheeze, and his nearly purple nose was peeling, but he seemed in decent shape. "Oh, I'm no one. Not like what you mean"

"You're here. You have to be someone."

"I have money. Billions. All stocks. That sort of thing. Nothing much to brag about."

"I see." My Mistress stared, unimpressed. "I guess what they say is true. Money *can* buy you anything. Nice meeting you, seventy-one. Remember, outside of here, you don't know me. Let's keep it that way."

His smile fell and his top lip peeled back angrily. I rushed to catch back up as a curse left my Mistress. She slammed the side of her fist into one of the apartment walls, not slowing until we passed a good ten rooms.

"People should learn to keep their mouths shut. I'm not *her* when I'm here. Not to them. *Not ever.*"

She put in a card, pushing the door open. Her eyes searched the space, clearly looking for the other slave she bought. I followed behind, still giving her distance as she swept into the bedroom. At her smile, I watched her transform completely. The straightness of her full lips curved up, and her face softened from the hard angles of her high cheekbones. When I took another step forward, I regretted it instantly. Light green eyes shot to me, and I was clearly looking at the most attractive guy I'd ever seen in person. Brown hair was on the shorter side, and he could have easily been an actor himself. His shoulders were wide, and muscle was thick and defined over every inch I could see above the gray sweatpants he wore.

As fast as his eyes came to me, they left, dismissing me as the no one I was. My Mistress's glare was back on me, but she was heading to him, lowering to kneel before his shackled frame.

"You did good. The weakling doesn't exist to you. Not until I say. Do you understand?"

The man rose to his knees as if he were under some sort of

spell, not able to go further because of the shackles restraining one hand and one foot. "Yes, Mistress."

"You see no one but me. You love me. *Adore me.* I'm the only one who means anything to you, and you obey my every need and desire. With you, I will lack for nothing. You promised to worship me. It's time to begin."

MISTRESS B-0003

"*G*et in or else you get shackled.*"*
   The words repeated in my head as fingers trailed through my wet hair. I could so clearly see myself pushing the blonde inside the closet, not able to look at her another second. My stomach had flipped at the action, and I had tried to block out all emotion. It would take a little time, but I wouldn't feel bad for my behavior. I had a role to play. Being a Mistress was new. I was the owner of slaves now. To remain at the Gardens and get what I wanted, this had to be done. The less I had to look at her, the better.

   The weakling may have not been my first choice for a virgin, but truthfully, looks had nothing to do with what I needed. Sure, she was pretty and young. Still, it wasn't her beauty I desired. I had my own appearance to worry about, and with her, I'd finally get what I dreamed. Not just a wise tale about the fountain of youth, but a craving I had for as long as I could remember: *blood.*

   To feel it on my skin was power. It was lust. To be soaked in it…a fantasy, but not for long. Would it be adrenalizing like I'd heard? Blissful like with the blood masks? I liked that, but I'd never had one from a virgin before. It was supposedly a stronger sensation. What had Jillian called it: a high like no other? Yes, I needed it all, but in time. First, the masks as I allowed myself to adjust to this life, and then...*the important part.* In the meantime, I would stay as detached as possible. To both of them.

Cold. Confident.

"Okay, stop."

My eyes cracked open as fingers halted in my hair. After my fun at the auction, I had my male slave shower me. He'd even surprised me by going down on me, but he stopped from moving further on his own after I'd had my orgasm. I like that he recognized I wasn't in the mood for more. It wasn't going to take much to train him. He read me well. Too well, if I wanted to be honest, but I liked the intensity he had, studying me. He was so eager to please and make me happy just like they said in the classes; I just had to keep it that way. To be soft or let him have more of me would defeat any sense of ownership I carried. I was his Mistress, not his girlfriend. Men always seemed to blur the line and try to take more than I wanted to give. With him being a blank slate[1], I technically didn't have to worry about that, but I'd make sure I wouldn't let that happen just in case.

Sitting, I yawned, fixing the robe as I walked to the vanity just outside the bathroom door. It was feet from the end of my bed, and I didn't miss my slave's movement from the pillow to the bottom of the mattress. He was waiting. Not relaxing like I thought he would.

Point for him.

I pulled out the chair, picking up my brush as I glanced up at him in the mirror. He went to stand but stopped at my hard shake. Frozen, his eyes studied mine. He was thinking he upset me somehow. The slave was questioning himself after my abrupt stop to his affection. And that's what he'd been trying to give when he was playing with my hair. I knew expressions and how to wear every single one flawlessly, and he was perplexed.

"Mistress?"

"No."

I left it at that. I would not give him a reason for my distance. He had to accept my decisions no matter what they were.

Minutes went by as I brushed my long hair. I went to stand, stopping as I glanced back at his reflection. I spun on the rectangular stool, facing him. What had his name been before he came here? What was his personality like before he was taken? Hobbies? What were his dreams? The questions registered, but I pushed them away. It was pointless to know, but it could give me insight into his mindset, which might help more than the generic profile I'd read through when I chose him. But would it be okay to bring those up? Surely, it wouldn't mess him up somehow. It's not like they warned us not to bring up their past.

"This robe I'm wearing is wet. There's an ivory silk night-gown set hanging at the back of the closet. Retrieve it and dress me."

There wasn't an ounce of hesitation as the slave pushed to his feet and headed for the closet door. I stood, stopping at the bottom of the bed so I could watch him. The space wasn't anywhere as big as my closet in my Hollywood penthouse, but I also didn't have much of a wardrobe here either. That was something I needed to change. I didn't have many options for clothing if I wanted to explore the city and actually participate in one of the many events they hosted.

Head up, my slave stepped over the curled-up girl, not even glancing down as he took the hanger from the wooden pole and turned back to face me. As he returned, he was already removing the ivory silk top and unclamping the matching shorts. My hand came up causing him to slow.

"Do you know how to braid?"

I lifted my arms, waiting as he brought the top up to slide it down my chest. He quickly grabbed the shorts, bending to allow me to step into them. Teeth sunk into his bottom lip, and he slowed at my lower thighs, tracing one of his index fingers over my skin. As quick as he stole the touch, he blinked through his mistake, sliding the shorts to my hips.

"I know how to braid, Mistress. Not very well, but I will practice until I make you happy."

"Good. I want you to braid my hair, and come morning, you'll take it out. But you will not brush it. That is a treat you haven't earned yet. Maybe in time you'll be so lucky." I adjusted the top, fixing it to hug my breasts, showing how displeased I was that he hadn't done it first. *"Or maybe not."*

Dismissing him, I stepped around his tall frame, gazing into the closet at the helpless heap on my floor. She was awake, but she wasn't moving much.

"Weakling, if you have to go to the bathroom or take a shower, do it now. Once I go to bed, you will not wake me. Not ever. Is that understood?"

"Yes, Mistress."

"There are two dressers in the back of the closet. One is full of my slave's clothes; the other is mine. You can have a pair of my panties from my drawer and a T-shirt from his. You will keep yourself covered at all times. Is that clear?"

"Yes, Mistress."

"Hurry up and do whatever you need."

The girl flew to her feet, disappearing to the back of the closet, only to race for the bathroom. I sat on the edge of the bed, trying not to grind my teeth through the anger at even having to deal with her. I didn't like females. Not really, and especially not ones like this crying, cowering girl here. I saw myself in them. I saw my mother. Weak. Both of us back in those days. Pathetic. Punching bags. Playthings for predators, and she allowed it. Even gave me to them if it helped to support us.

My fists gripped into the comforter as I stared ahead. All I could see was white metal from the old trailer we'd lived in. It wasn't even a big one, more of a travel trailer size, sporting one bedroom in the back, and the table that I used that turned into a bed. But he didn't get me inside that day. No...I didn't make it that far. I hadn't even made it to the front door before I felt hands grip my hips.

"Your momma says you got the rent this month, Char. Is she right?" One of his arms slid around my waist, locking in tight as the other tried forcing my legs apart. I threw my body off to the side to try to break his hold, but I'd been here before. There was no winning. There was also nowhere to live if I didn't do this. Could I, again? Could I endure letting our landlord touch me down there as I jacked him off? I was a virgin. That was one thing I had going for me. That didn't excuse my mouth, ass, or hand. I wanted as far from this old, stinky man as I could get, and ultimately, I had.

Shame was empowering. Life changing for me. Getting caught with Mr. Gorbes by my neighborhood crush shouldn't have made such an impact, but for me it scorched the fighter I had inside. It brought her to life making her run right to the one place littered with more predators than that rundown trailer park, but I made it, and I grew stronger. I found my backbone and worked on my self-esteem. I also grew angry as fuck, and with each man who touched me, the festering rage built. It still was locked away inside, whispering sweet nothings of murder and mayhem as I tried to kill that weak little girl I used to be.

"Mistress?"

The whisper was so light it barely pulled me from the outside of the trailer. I blinked the memories away, taking in the brush and hairband my slave held. I hadn't even seen him get it from my vanity. This girl couldn't be here for much longer. Not when I knew I owned her very weak existence. And I wasn't helpless anymore. I wouldn't be associated with such low vibrations or have it around me. Nor...would I look at it.

"Bring the chair for me. You'll sit on the bed."

29

Happiness. Although the slave kept his face straight, I could see how excited he was to serve. It was a mistake with my mood.

I stood, letting him sit down the stool. I grabbed the brush, crushing his feelings as I ran it through my hair a few times. When I tossed it on the bed and divided my hair into three parts, only then did I sit on the stool and wait for him. It didn't take long.

My hair disappeared from both shoulders, and I felt the part in the middle of my back lift as he began to attempt his braid.

"What is your name?"

A pause behind me.

"Slave eighty-eight."

"I'm aware of that," I said, dryly. "I mean your real name. The one you had before you came here."

Silence. It lasted for so long as my hair weaved that I almost turned around.

"Mark Reston."

"It says you were Ivy League, and that you're really smart."

He shifted, moving towards the end of my long hair.

"Yale. Two years. Biomedical Sciences."

"Interesting." He finished putting in the hairband, and I turned, seeing the conflicting emotions on his face. "Did you enjoy it?" At my hand pressing into his chest, the slave laid back on the bed. I crawled up, straddling his waist. The moment my hands flattened over his muscled pecs, his eyes shut in pleasure.

"I did. I loved it. I haven't thought about those days in a long time."

The last was whispered. My fingers roamed from shoulder to shoulder as the shower turned on in the background. I let myself explore his skin, moving over the muscles. The hardness from him nestled between my legs didn't escape me, but I ignored his cock, instead, increasing and decreasing my touch.

"Have you ever been in love, slave?"

Light green met me as he opened his eyes.

"I thought I was once, but it wasn't love."

"No?"

His head shook. "More admiration. She was a hard worker and very smart. That appealed to me, but that's as far as it went. I don't think I ever even talked to her."

Where I expected a smile at the memories, he gave none, blinking his past away only to smile as he looked back up to me.

"What else would my Mistress like to know?"

"What was your personality like? How did you dress before you were taken? You were in a medical gown in your profile."

"Normal? Jeans, sweaters. T-shirts when it warmed up. I guess like you'd picture how any college kid dressed. I was boring. Learning was my life. I meant to make something of myself. I was determined to rise above the way I was raised."

The words were sobering and a mirror to myself, but they weren't the entire truth concerning him. "I see." My hands spanned over his chest, taking in his physique. "Were you always this fit?"

He laughed, surprising me. It sounded so normal. So real, as if he wasn't programmed at all. "Not exactly. I was okay, but this helped me keep my mind." His eyebrows drew in. "Is it too much for you?"

"No, I like it. I expect you to stay this way. I have a very strict diet. You will keep one as well."

Relief was obvious as the muscles underneath me relaxed.

"My body is yours. I'll get as big or as small as you want. I want to be your ideal slave. The perfect specimen you can create."

"Create." I lifted, crawling from the bed as I paced. My slave did have a point. One that I hadn't given much thought to. Sure, his looks were exactly what I had in mind for a dream slave. Hell, who was I fooling, he surpassed them, but what else did I want? I was so curious to discover who he was that I hadn't given much thought to who I'd like him to become. And that was

31

up to me. He had to dress with what I bought him. Eat what I wanted him to. Do whatever I said. Why wouldn't he appear the way I wanted, too?

"You're fascinating when you're deep in thought."

My eyes cut over. "And you're interrupting my genius, *Genius*. You're a smart one. Tell me what I want. If you were to profile me as Charlotte, the celebrity, who would be my ideal arm candy/bodyguard?"

My slave's head shook. "Arm candy." His gaze swept down as he thought. "Ask me about nanorobots or gene therapy, and I may be able to help you out. When it comes to celebs, I'm lost, Mistress. If I were to guess though." His brow creased through the concentration. "Most celebrities I know like the bad boys. The ones covered in tattoos. They're either drummers or rappers. Some, I guess, marry the rich bankers, but I don't see you wanting to get tied down with a suit. You're bold. No amount of arm candy could outshine your beauty, so therefore you wouldn't feel threatened by that. It would actually enhance your aura and make you appear even more irresistible. As for a bodyguard, I guess most are covered too, just for different reasons." He stopped, staring at me so hard I almost felt as if he could see into my very thoughts. "I guess the real question is, who are you? Are you Charlotte the celebrity, or are you Charlotte the Mistress? Is she the same person, or are you here to find out?"

MOO88

I was always usually pretty good at knowing when to keep my mouth shut, but this voice in my head had me questioning everything. I couldn't get a read on my Mistress, and it was driving me crazy. One minute I felt I could speak honestly, and the next she grew cold out of nowhere. I was so confused, but desperate not to screw this up. I couldn't lose her. Not just because that meant my death, but because for some strange reason, I actually wanted to see how this would go. She was distant and angry a lot, but there was a softness to her when she dropped her guard, and it was something this new slave part of me needed.

"What is taking the weakling so long? Did she fall asleep in there?"

A growl left her as she dismissed my question. I stayed on the edge of the bed, waiting for what she wanted from me next. It took all my willpower not to focus on the way her hard nipples pressed into the ivory silk fabric as she paced, but so far I was doing well.

"I'm hungry. I didn't eat."

I stood at her nearly inaudible whispers. It was thoughts spoken aloud, nothing more, but I was ready.

"Would you like me to check to see what you have? I'm an okay cook. I can make you something."

A long moment went by.

"Slave, come here."

I took two steps to get to her. When she pointed to the ground, I lowered to my knees. There was such recognition on her face as she held to my jaw and turned my face from side to side. More incoherent mumbling left her as she let go and stepped back, scanning over my body.

"I think you're right on your first assessment. I do see the appeal to the bad boy, but not why I thought. I…"

Fear. Why it flashed in her eyes, I wasn't sure, but the new slave in me felt anger rise up again, and the need to protect my life, *her life*, had me almost reaching out.

"Looks don't define a person. I know that but they do alter perceptions." Her eyes cut back to me as she continued to pace. "You really had me thinking over my life and over who all I've surrounded myself with. They made me feel safe. So much so, I've forgotten what it's like to be alone. I wasn't allowed to bring bodyguards here. It's one reason I wanted and needed you. I read your past. You had a job as a bouncer part-time in college, so you know how to protect. And you grew up fighting. You weren't just a nerdy schoolboy. You had another side. Right?"

I blinked through her words, barely even recalling what she spoke of. Had I done that? Fuzzy images were barely reachable as I pressed my palm into my temple. I couldn't remember that part. Not really, which was aggravating. Some things were crystal clear while others were almost gone completely.

"Slave, I think you're a good fit for me, but if you looked the part it could help. If one looks scary enough, or are at least intimidating, they repel. I could use that for situations like today."

"Today?"

Fuck. Had I growled out that word? I was failing miserably in my duties, and it was only the first day. The fact that my Mistress went into explaining left me more than surprised.

"Some old guy. He recognized me and thought he'd try to strike up a conversation even though it's against the rules. I don't want to have to worry about that. It was one of the main reasons I embraced the idea of this place. Anonymity. I came here to escape that part of myself. At least to an extent. I wanted this to be secret. *My secret.* I'm aware people will recognize me, but I want them to leave me alone and let me do my thing down here without hounding me like everyone does on the outside world."

"And if I look intimidating, no one will bother you."

"Exactly," she breathed out.

My own mind raced at her implications. Not the fact that I assumed she meant to make me look like the tattooed bad boy bodyguard, but because she planned to let me leave this apartment with her. Had I picked up on that, correctly? We'd been so prepared for death, I never imagined actually facing a life here. Even when she mentioned bodyguard, it still hadn't processed I'd be leaving this apartment. Why was I not able to think clearly? Everything in my mind revolved around the moment and her. Not the future or the past unless there was reason for me to think about it. Only the present.

Flashes of the place we were in came flooding into me from my tour. We were in some strange sort of city. A real place with shopping and restaurants. Being her bodyguard meant I was to stay with her wherever she went, so it had to be that. I'd be living here, actually having a real life. Right? Think!

Thump-thump. My pulse was racing as I tried to control my excitement. More hope. More bliss. More…infatuation and gratitude for my Mistress.

"If it makes you happy, it makes me happy."

"Of course it does, slave. Go get me a yogurt." The attitude was back, but I didn't miss her voice softening at the end. "Did you eat dinner, or did they not feed you before the auction? I can't have you losing any size. I need you to scare people, or at least keep them away."

Warmth flooded through at her hidden concern. Had this been the old me, perhaps I would have walked over and thrown her on the bed; climbed on top of her and snuffed out that brat she loved to embrace. But I wasn't the old me. I wasn't even sure I was correct on the assessment of thinking that's how I'd been. I barely remembered, but I could feel it now. Feel that roll of the wild. It beckoned me to dip my toes into it. To test her to see just how much she truly wanted to be in control, but that was forbidden. It'd probably get me killed.

"They fed me, Mistress. Give me a moment, I'll grab your yogurt."

"Grab one for you anyway. No, grab you two." The bathroom door opened, and she rolled her eyes. "Add another. Weakling can't starve to death on me yet. And a water." Charlotte pointed to the floor next to the shackles. "Weakling, sit. I won't chain you up yet, but you will be restrained while I sleep. I don't trust you not to run."

My Mistress's voice faded as I went through the dark living room. I flipped on the light, opening the stainless-steel refrigerator. The thing was completely stocked with vegetables of every kind. There were fruits, water, and power drinks. There were even protein bars, a carton of eggs, tons of yogurts. Most of the food rested in fancy Tupperware, keeping them fresh, but it was the organization that shocked me. Had Charlotte done this, or had someone else? Her. It had to have been. I needed to remember the order. It was perfection, and I didn't want to screw anything up.

"*Slave.*" The yell had me grabbing four yogurts and a water. I searched through the drawers, finally finding the spoons. As I jogged back to the room, I nearly swore under my breath. The fucking light.

"As my Mistress wanted." I handed her the yogurt, spoon, and water, not even looking over to the girl as I tossed the small container and a spoon in her vicinity. "And mine." I said, lifting my two. "But I have to go back to turn off the light. Do you need anything else while I'm in there?"

Full lips twisted, and she narrowed her eyes. "Actually, yes, one of the packs of granola. The vanilla and almond. Not the ones with the chocolate chunks; it's too late for that. That'll be for breakfast."

"I'll remember your preferences."

"Yes, you will, but we won't be eating here in the morning. We're going out. I have some shopping to do, and I want to inquire on a tattoo artist. I'm not even sure this place has one."

Her words stopped me in my tracks. Was I getting to go out so soon? It almost didn't seem real after the last eleven months of mainly staying inside one room. Was I ready for that? For the people? For...her? What if I messed up? What if I made her angry?

Calm and stay composed.

I cleared my throat at the voice, pulling myself together. "They have one. I saw it on my tour." I thought back, trying to recall the whereabouts. "I believe it's two blocks down the main road, to the left. It was next to a seafood bar and grill."

"A bar and grill. Hmm. Great, we know where we're going for lunch." She stopped, her head tilting as she took me in. "You're nervous. That's not very reassuring to me, slave."

Straightening, the anger came back, more at myself than anything.

"*There*. Right there. Hold that look."

"Look?"

Something close to fascination had my Mistress tossing her unopened yogurt and drink to the bed as she headed towards me.

37

I kept the anger present, testing the emotion as she pulled me deeper into the room and began to circle around.

"You can be feared. A beautiful fear. And sexy, but…there has to be something more. Depth. Truth." She came back around to face me. "Death. You won't be a killer until I make you one. That aura has to be strong. It'll project like an alarm to anyone that gets close. We're far from that man. This person…this slave…that's not him yet, but if you're good. If you can act to the point where you believe it, we might have the perfect man. Slave," she corrected. "Man-slave. You get it. Get out and turn off that light. And don't forget my granola."

Man-slave. More than a slave. A man. *Her man.* Or, no, she'd said perfect man.

I threw open the pantry door, scanning the shelves until I grabbed the package. Perfect man. That's what she wanted out of me: a hot, dark, tattooed protector that would kill for her. *Kill…*if she meant anyone other than slaves, that would get me a death sentence. We were already warned it was certain death if we attacked a Master, but if something was happening to my Mistress to where she needed me, I could defend her. Yes. I could kill for her.

Hitting the light, I entered the room, catching the weakling skittering across the floor to return to her seat from the small trash can by the door. Instinct brought my eyes right where they belonged, right to Charlotte. The moment I got to the bed and handed her the small circular package of granola, she pointed to the wall.

"You'll eat right there and then you'll shower and return. There's extra blankets and pillows in the closet. You'll sleep against that wall. The bed is too good for you right now. You'll get your place beside me when you earn it. If I awake at any time and you're not there, you're in trouble."

"Yes, Mistress."

Damn. Disappointment weighed heavily in my stomach. Had

I thought I'd be able to be close to her? Smell her? Be there for her if she wanted me? Shit. She didn't want sex. Not yet, but I sure as hell did. After the taste I had of her earlier, I could have spent hours with my face buried between her legs. She made the softest sounds. The sweet moans echoed in my ears making me harder than I'd been all day. And there were moments I constantly had to reign in the lust. Every time she touched me it was pure agony. I wasn't sure I'd ever be used to it after so long. What I did know was now that I'd gotten contact, I couldn't go without it.

I sat down with my yogurt, keeping my stare on my food as I went through the tiny servings like they were nothing. I could do better. It was the only thing that kept repeating in my head. It may take time, but I could do this.

Standing to throw the yogurts away, I stopped in my tracks at my Mistress's look. Should I have announced my sudden move? Had I done it too aggressively? I was aggravated at myself for not winning her over more than I had.

"I'm sorry. I'm going to get some clothes and take a shower now. Can I get something for you before I go, Mistress?"

"Not yet. Take your shower but try to hurry. It's late. I'm getting tired."

I nodded, taking a step towards her and outstretching my hand for the empty yogurt container. She looked down, blinking back the surprise. She did appear tired as she handed it over and leaned back to rest against the pillow.

"Lock the weakling up on your way." She yawned. "And grab the 'thing' a blanket. We don't want her ruining our big day tomorrow by having to search her out."

"Yes, Mistress."

By the time I got the extra pillows and blankets and was laying mine out in my spot, I dreaded going to the other slave. I could ignore her all day long, but I wasn't immune to her presence. And I knew her fate. It rested with me.

39

Nearly groaning, I headed over, dumping the blanket down next to her.

"Foot and hand. Hurry up."

"Why are you so mad at me? Everyone's so...mean. I don't want to be here." I wouldn't look at her as she whispered. I wouldn't feel her fear or pain. She didn't exist. The slave was no one. A ghost. She was already dead.

I snatched her ankle, snapping the shackle around it. When I went to reach for her hand, she was already holding it out. I locked her in, storming back into the closet. There was so much feeling pounding my insides. Where I usually worked out to burn my energy, it was never this strong. Besides, I couldn't do that here. Not right now.

Two dressers sat at the back of the closet, and I opened one, seeing it full of sexy lingerie and panties. The sight of the delicate lace, silk, and satin had me trailing my digit over them. They were my Mistresses...and she was mine. I'd see these on her. *Charlotte Wyce.* If I was lucky, I'd get to take them off. Nothing about that made me feel bad for being a slave. Charlotte Wyce. *The* Charlotte Wyce. And mine. *Us.*

Shutting the drawer, I moved to the other dresser, pulling out a pair of briefs. I threw them back in, grabbing just a pair of cotton pajama bottoms that had a plaid print. Cotton. Nothing fancy. Nothing high-class. Slave. Me. But *her* slave.

I hadn't even realized I was smiling until it fell from my face at her watching me. Maybe I figured she was already asleep, but she was waiting. She needed me, and she'd told me to hurry.

"I'll be quick, Mistress."

"You better."

WO166

I hated this life. How could a slave like me turn their back on one of their own? It made no sense and infuriated me to no end. The guy wouldn't even look at me. He refused to meet my eyes or see what my face looked like. Each time he passed or turned the smallest amount my way, I wanted to wave toward him to try to get his attention. I know she said to ignore me, but weren't we in this together?

No. Who was I kidding. I wasn't even considered a slave, but worse, a weakling. And he had the dresser, not me. The guy's spot was more cemented, and why wouldn't it be? He was a God turned slave, and she was an angel turned Mistress. They were made in heaven but found each other in hell. What were the odds?

Water poured in the background, and I tried to get comfortable with the cold metal latched around my wrist and leg. I'd never get used to this. If it didn't mean I'd die, maybe I would have prayed for something to remove them, but they were testament my heart still beat, and I wanted to live.

"Is that something I see other than fear, slave?"

My Mistress's voice had me glancing to the end of the bed where she had her head propped up.

"I'm annoyed."

"I can see that. What makes you angrier, your situation or my slave's lack of attention towards you?"

Could I be honest? Did I have anything else to really lose? She was going to kill me anyway. I didn't think she'd do it tonight.

"Both."

"We deal with whatever the Fate's throw at us. That's what we women do. We rise or we fall during our time here. You, dear, are the fallen."

"I didn't choose to be taken."

"Ooh, listen to that. She has some spark to her." The Mistress turned to sit up on the edge of the bed. "You're wrong. You chose it one way or another. You may not be aware of it, but your choices determined your outcome. The fact that you haven't grown stronger or learned from them is what gets me. You should be tougher after all this, but you're not. Fallen. There's no hope for you. You gave up a long time ago."

My mouth clamped closed because I knew she was right. How many times had I replayed the moments that led up to my abduction? Too many to count. Had I not ditched school, I would have never been walking down that road to go home. I wouldn't have been taken. And it wasn't just that. There were moments I could have fought. Times I could have done things differently. I took the easy way out. I didn't stand up to anyone or face confrontation. Fear. It ruled me. Maybe it always would.

"There it is. You see. I knew if you were honest with yourself, you'd understand."

"I do. What I don't understand is why I'm here, or why you're here. You're going to kill me. I know that part. The 'why' is what I want to know. Don't I at least deserve to know the truth?"

She laughed, sarcastically. "No. *Because its none of your business*. As it happens, it's your lucky day. You want the answer to why I wanted you here…it's about to present itself. You want truth. You can't handle it, weakling, but you're about to see anyway."

The water turned off and the terror returned a billion-fold. I was sitting, scooting to the wall as my Mistress's tall frame stood. She couldn't have been more than five-feet-eight-inches, but she could have been seven feet for how much she terrified me.

"If you piss on my carpet, so help me, you'll lick it up until it's gone."

"What will you have him do to me?"

What seemed like years went by before she crossed her arms over her chest.

"You're going to bleed for me." The door opened, but the Mistress didn't pause in speaking. "He's going to cut along your forearm, and then he's going to paint my face with your blood. That's what he's going to do to you." She turned her attention to the male slave, holding out a small knife. And like I knew would happen, he stepped forward to take it without thought.

The Mistress sat down not a foot from me. If I could have run, I would have. All I could do was curl more into the wall as she stared me down.

"If you fight, he'll cut deep. Today you may live. Tomorrow night when I want him to do it again, you may not. If you do this peacefully and submit every night, you'll make it another day."

"My blood?"

My voice cracked as her stare at me remained stoic. Her eyes swept to the slave as he knelt, grabbing hard to my free arm. It was tense, but I allowed him to pull it close to him without too much of a fight. After all, I was torn on what I should do. I didn't trust him not to hit some major vein and kill me. But if I really fought, I was as good as dead.

"Shallow," the Mistress snapped. "Unless she fights you."

"Please. Mistress, please. I don't want this. Please." A cold hardness pushed along the middle, and I cried out as a sharp pain caused me to jolt in his tight hold. The burning only went down a half inch before the metal stopped.

"Perfect, slave." But the guy didn't need praise. He was already using the pad of his thumb to smear crimson over her face like the robot he was. It was so bright against her skin, it horrified me. I kept trying to scoot back, to pull my arm away from him, but there was nowhere for me to go. Escape was impossible. So, where did that leave me? Here, bleeding out for this psycho-actress, or did I risk it all and suffer the consequences?

MISTRESS B-0003

ad I expected him to balk? To look at me horrified and judge me? I told myself I didn't care even if he did, but a part of me still wasn't used to people knowing my secret. My slave's lack of reaction had me letting out a sigh I didn't even know I was holding. It was the first night. The hardest one, if I wanted to be honest, but now Mark knew. If I could read him right, a small part of him maybe even liked it. Or maybe it was wishful thinking.

"A little more, Mistress." His lids lowered through the concentration as he continued to apply. "May I speak?"

I turned enough to face him. It had my slave's hand stopping just short of my jaw. There was a nervousness but something more. Something I couldn't read, and I didn't like it. My insecurities came back. Maybe even ones that had led me to this place to begin with.

"I'm your agent, and I'm being honest with you, Charlotte. They said no. You're too old for that role."

"That's what you said about the last one I suggested as well."

"Because that's what they told me. It wasn't my choice. You

know I'll do whatever you ask, but I can't make them star you in the film if you're not what they're looking for."

"Make them! I'm not too old. I don't look it." I'd stopped, glancing over to the mirror. Did I look old? I was thirty-eight. I took good care of myself, but was I considered old?

A yell had poured from me, and I stormed out. "Fuck them. Fuck you all." And then my search had begun. It started with research and reaching out to my connections. Then I'd been introduced to Jillian. She was the one who eventually mentioned this place. Now...this.

"What, slave?" The words pushed through my clenched teeth. He swallowed hard, using his towel to press against the weakling's wound. "Just say it."

"There are other means in association with this that you could use if you want. Techniques I would be more than happy to learn to do for you, if you'd allow me the training. I'm smart. I can do it. I'm here to serve you."

My slave's words took a moment to break through. Where I expected him to criticize me or make some excuse as to why I didn't need this, he wasn't. He wanted to help. To learn.

"What sort of things are you talking about? Not plastic surgery or filler. I won't do that; I refuse."

His head shook, and he eased me to stand. When I let him lead me to the edge of the bed, he gave me back the knife.

"You're aware of estheticians?"

"Of course."

"Have you been to one?"

A finger trailed over my wrist, soft, barely there. I jerked my hand away, seeing Mark's eyes flare. Had he even realized he was touching me?

"I went once. I didn't like the office. They were wrong." My lips tightened through my confession. "I had a friend, Jillian, who would send me trusted vials of blood and cream to apply. They've worked fairly well, but I was told the real thing works better. Not that I need any of it. I'm fine. I just…I want to see for myself if there's a difference."

"You're the most beautiful woman in the world. Not just to me, but to millions of people. For you to believe what we all know, you have to feel it. I can learn anything you want. Get me the machines and training, and I will do what those offices charge a fortune for. I've already studied and know the bulk of it. You'd never have to face anyone else again. You have me, and you can have it all. This," he said, motioning to the weakling, "*and* the treatment you don't want anyone to know about. Have you heard of the vampire facial?"

Staring at his enthusiastic face, I nodded. "I've had friends who've had them done."

"I can do that for you. Anything you desire can be yours, and it can be through me."

Silence filled the room as I glanced down at the floor in a daze. He did have a point. Everywhere I went ended up in the papers. I was lucky about protocol to get in this place, or else it wouldn't have been possible. People saw me enter the airport and take off on my private jet, but that's where it ended. I'd arrived in Denver for a stop, but when my jet took off again, I wasn't on it. I was in the underground system with military drivers who brought me here. Out in the real world, nothing was private, and I hated that.

"Let me think on it. Learning is a privilege. Prove to me you're worth that much investment."

He smiled, nodding. "I'm going to show you I'm the best slave for you. No one will ever be as devoted. You'll see."

"You're nervous."

"I'm observing."

"You're nervous, and you're making me nervous," I whispered, nearly growling through the word. "Do I need to take you home to be with the weakling, and go on my own?"

The wounded expression that swept over my slave's face disappeared just as fast.

"How am I supposed to protect you if I'm at home? *I'm staying.*"

"Oh, are you? Are you the Mistress, here?"

The authority that had been in his tone had him opening his mouth, only to close it. He knew he'd made a mistake. The shock was clear, but I couldn't dismiss the ping of lust it had stirred either. Men were a dime a dozen and rarely any appealed, but the ones who had, were the ones who could put me in my place. I needed that from time to time, and if Mark could do that, I may be in trouble. It went against what I wanted him for. Unless he could be both, but I wasn't sure that was possible...or even good with his training.

"Forgive me, Mistress. I apologize. I'm trying my best. There's just so many people. We can barely move without someone almost bumping into you."

"So don't let them. If you're my protector, do your job. Besides, I don't think it will always be like this. It's opening weekend and we've all been waiting almost a year to get in here. Give it a few months and we'll probably never have to deal with this again."

My slave's brows drew in. "How long will you be staying? I know you have a life on the outside. Will you be here much longer? Will you come often?"

Sadness. I tried to ignore it and stay detached as was suggested by the pamphlet, but I didn't miss the way his emotion stirred me. I kept my stare ahead, towards the elevator.

"I'm on an extended vacation at the moment. I just finished filming, so you have some time."

His face relaxed. He kept quiet, but he scanned the crowds, making sure no one got too close. It was in the way he snaked his arm around my lower back to hold onto my hip. A slight pull here. A sway there. A few times his fingers even flexed against me, adding the most delicious pressure as we made our way out of the main building and into the outside city. The moment the elevator opened and we stepped off, we both stood rooted into place.

"Son of a bitch." My slave cleared his throat. "I'm sorry, Mistress."

"Son of a bitch is right. Look at all these people. Do you think we can even make it through the road?"

A big swallow, but I saw him stand taller, widening his shoulders as he led us forward to weave through the crowd.

Loud street music played off in the distance and the smell of different foods wafted through. There were lines into some boutiques, and what I assumed was a slave dressed in a yellow wrap, yelled out numbers.

"Forty-two! You're up, Forty-two!"

"That's me."

An old man in a suit surged from a nearby bistro table, taking a bloodied spiked club from a rack as he went inside. Just below the numerous tools was more blood and chunks of what looked to be hair and scalp.

I scanned the name of the shop, nearly running into the couple in front of me as I did.

The Batting Cage

Screams were already coming from the place, but they grew louder as solid thumps began making an impact from inside.

"No way. Is...Is he?"

But my slave didn't answer. I turned just in time to see his arm shoot out, blocking some large man from crashing right into me. The impact was so powerful it caused the man to spin to the side right into a group of others making their way in the opposite direction. Yells went up and I grabbed his wrist, pulling Mark deeper into the crowd, but it only got worse. The smell of alcohol was almost suffocating. The noise level from the voices and music made me want to cover my ears. I kept stealing glances to my slave, but we both were so focused on making our way through without getting trampled, it was almost impossible.

"Look at that ass! Fuck, baby, come back this way."

"Take it. Take her! Right there on the table. Bend her over!"

Moans, screams. They mingled with the noise, prominent as we passed what looked like an old town saloon. It was getting so hot I could barely breathe. Sweat covered my skin, and I felt myself reach for Mark's black shirt. It was practically soaked and sticking to his muscled body as he shoved out his hand again.

"Fuck this. Mistress." His eyes were narrowed but determined as he leaned in. I could see his internal battle as his gaze penetrated mine, and I knew the moment I saw a darker side of him win. He looked at my lips but licked his own. "Forgive me, but I'm going to have to take the punishment on this one. I'm getting you the fuck out of here."

Before I could argue, he threw me over his shoulder, sending people flying. He pushed anyone in the vicinity out of his way as he took us further into the road. He turned left, slamming his fist brutally into a stumbling man who was falling right into us. When he finally threw open the black metal door of the tattoo place, cold air rushed against me, and he put me to my feet. All I could do was stare up at him in nothing short of shock. Awe. *Need.*

"Dirty Anchor. One of you looking to get inked up?"

My slave smiled, facing the man. I couldn't. I was still stuck on his gorgeous face. Had he become more attractive, or was I losing my mind? No one had ever done anything like that for me. Sure, bodyguards came close, but they hadn't held that sort of... ferocity. It was inside him, reeling me in as if it had truly hooked me. Who was this man locked away? This...power he held? I liked it way more than I should.

"Me. My Mistress wishes for me to be covered in tattoos. She'll be choosing what I get."

"I believe I should be the one telling him this." I forced anger to take over my enamored features. "Sit your ass down. You're in trouble for that shit you just pulled. I don't believe I said I needed help."

A pout. It appeared, but he sat down on a black velvet chair. I turned to the tattoo artist, taking in his own tattoos. There was a cross just off to the side of his right eye. Ink covered his neck and arms in what looked like a Japanese theme. Black words and art even covered his hands and what part of his legs I could see from below his shorts.

"Are you familiar with the rock star, Pistol Stephens?"

The artist laughed. "He was in here not an hour ago."

"Perfect. Then when I say cover him, you know what I mean. Give me heaven and hell. Heaven on the back, hell where I can see it. History. Dark gothic with a romantic twist. Religion. Chapels. Gargoyles. That sort of thing. Freestyle it. I don't care. I need it immediately. Neck down. Oh." I pointed to my face, where he had the cross. "CW."

"Charlotte Wyce. Got it."

"What would you like done today?"

I glanced at my slave only to turn back to him. "As much as you can. Start with the face and work your way down. I have shopping to do. Text me on your last hour and I will return to retrieve him. If he gives you *any* trouble feel free to text me too. I'll take care of it." I took out my special Mistress phone I'd received from the Gardens. "What's your number?"

As I entered the digits and texted him, I didn't even feel my slave move in behind me. I turned to threaten him, only to crash right into his chest. His finger settled under my chin as his other arm wrapped around, righting me. He brought my face up, and I saw the power again behind his eyes as they bore into mine.

"You can't go out there on your own. It's not safe."

"You listen to what you're told." I slapped his hand down, putting distance between us. Having a part of him becoming so dominant wasn't good for my persona of a Mistress. I felt myself soften. *I wanted to give in.* Even if for the smallest amount of time. "Best behavior, slave. I better not hear a single thing about you acting up or I'll buy a crop, beat you with it, and keep you in my closet for days. Do you want that?"

"Maybe not the closet." At my pause, he tightened his jaw. "No, Mistress."

"Are you going to listen?"

"Yes, Mistress."

"He has my number. If you need me, text or call. I'll make it back here when I can." I glanced over my shoulder. "How long do you think?"

The tattoo artist checked his watch. It was still early, just after nine and we'd already eaten breakfast. "Come back around seven tonight."

"Seven." I repeated it, nodding, but not liking him gone that long. "You'll need to eat. I'll be back in a few hours to bring you food and check on you. *Behave.*"

M0088

Seeing myself in a mirror again was going to take some getting used to. I didn't know this man. Not the one under the new tattoos, or the one who stared back. There'd been no way to see myself since I'd been taken. Glass was a risk to the slaves in their cells, and even the shower rooms had been empty aside from the facilities. This man. This stranger I'd turned into the last year, he had matured since his days back in college. The angles by my cheek bones were sharper. My jaw even appeared more defined. I looked...good underneath all this ink. Even better with it, but damn good.

Should I think that? Was I entitled to my looks?

We'd undergone so much training by the guards during our time locked away. Or maybe it was brainwashing. They taught us how to behave for the Masters and Mistresses. They repeated the rules to us over and over. Overtly, they tried erasing any form of humanity we held. Sometimes, they'd even hook us up to machines or put this weird thing on our heads, and I'd just wake up back in my room. I didn't know what happened, but my mind wouldn't let me dive too deep into it. I wasn't cut or injured. I was fine as far as I knew. We were objects. Nothing. Playthings for those of superior quality. It was truth. But here, now, maybe I was something? Charlotte chose me, and she was the most beautiful woman alive. That spoke volumes, didn't it?

"I'm late; I'm sorry."

The voice had me spinning from the mirror. I hadn't seen her since she brought me lunch. Whether my alertness came from the shaky tone or the fact it was *her*, I wasn't sure.

"*You're bleeding.*"

Had that deep voice been mine? I barely even heard it as I stalked in her direction. Blood was smeared under her nose, and her cheek was pink and slightly swollen. Even the seam along her gold blouse was torn. Before I could touch her, my Mistress's hand shot out as a warning. She was angry. Or maybe she was scared.

"It's still crazy out there." She took out her card, handing it to the tattoo artist as she pulled me deeper into the room to look at me. Her hand lifted, peeling back the clear wrap covering my neck. For long moments she scanned the dark shades. "I like it. Stop chewing on your damn lip. I've had a lot worse."

She finally looked up and met my eyes.

"What happened?"

"A drunk fool, that's what happened. He didn't see me, or maybe he didn't care as he overexpressively swung his stupid arms through the air. Idiots. All of them."

Despite knowing she was going to get angrier, I reached up, trailing my finger along the swollen part of her cheek.

"I'll take care of you when we get home."

No slap to my hand. No threat of the closet or a beating. Her lip quivered, and she left me there, heading back to the counter to retrieve her card. I caught up, listening to the tattoo artist finish up the last-minute instructions to my Mistress and apply the new wrap to my neck. It didn't take long before I was holding the door open as we began to leave. Was she limping?

"I got your cream. He expects you back tomorrow at the same time."

She couldn't disguise the fear in her tone. We rounded the turn, faced with the chaos all over again. I glanced at my Mistress, taking her by the bicep to pull her in. Her gaze met mine and she swallowed hard, her eyes filling with tears as she nodded. I felt whatever happened out here without me went beyond what she was telling me. Something bad transpired that knocked her into a mindset I hadn't seen on her before, and it enraged me. I lowered, barring my arm under her ass as I lifted her against the front of my body. To my surprise, her arms wrapped around my neck loosely, and the side of her face came to settle against mine. Wetness slid against my cheek and the heat boiled inside my chest as she shook through the silent sobs. Maybe people could see it. Maybe they sensed I was looking for someone to put through a wall. All I knew was someone hurt my Mistress, and if I wasn't a killer now, I could easily become one soon.

Shops blurred by. Sound faded to a dull roar. I took in every man I could see wondering if it were them. Praying she'd stop me and point them out. She didn't. Charlotte stayed glued to my body, allowing me to carry her all the way to the elevator. Silence followed us the entire ride up. She wasn't crying anymore, but her eyes were still red and swollen from how hard she had. My jaw was even still wet from her tears. A part of me loved to have her like this, but not at the price it had come. If she wasn't crying over me, I didn't want her crying at all.

"It suits you." She cleared her throat, sniffling. "The tattoos; your anger. You were made for this look."

"I'm assuming I don't get to know what really happened."

"I think your ego needs to drop another notch or two, Mr. Badass. There's nothing to say. I told you, it was a drunk asshole who was waving his hands around. I wasn't prepared."

"Waving around at first, before he saw you? What happened after that, he just continued?"

The elevator door opened, and Charlotte's eyes got so small through her glare, I was sure she was going to start beating me on the spot. Instead, she took off at a fast pace, heading down our hall. When she threw open the door and pushed me in, I was ready for her wrath. The door slammed shut, and she was shoving her hand hard into my chest.

"You are my protector. My slave. You are not my daddy, and you are *not* my boyfriend. You have one job and it's whatever the fuck I say. ***Down!***"

I'd barely budged two steps through all her pushing, but I lowered to kneel in the middle of the living room floor anyway. The sobs were back, and her anger was evident. She immediately held both sides of my face as she leaned in towards me.

"Do you hear what I'm telling you?"

"Yes, Mistress."

"Do you understand that you are my slave? That your job is to obey everything I say?"

"Yes, Mistress."

"Do I need to put you in the closet?"

"No."

At the look, I let out a breath.

"No, Mistress."

"Come shower me. It's almost ten, and I'm going to bed. I'm done with this day."

Again, she left, and again I caught up. Charlotte stormed from the closet with clothes in tow, still stomping her feet as she made her way into the bathroom. My eyes cut over in time to see the weakling smirking. *Enjoying and basking in my Mistress's pain.* The rage I projected wasn't intentional, but I knew when I'd jerked to a stop and glared in her direction, she felt every emotion that was boiling inside me. The girl immediately cowered, lowering her head as I started walking again and pushed the door open to join my Mistress. She stood there, waiting. Ready.

The moment I approached, she lifted her arms. I tried to ignore the tear on the blouse but didn't miss the dirt smeared further along the side. I hadn't seen that earlier.

"Hurry up. I hurt and I want to get clean."

One arm was straighter than the other. I tried to ignore it as I grabbed the hem of the shirt and lifted. Any other time, I would have seen full, beautiful breasts peeking through the nude lace bra. Not tonight. The large bruising over her ribs took over my sight, my focus, hell…my fucking world. *I did that by not being there to protect her. This was partly my fault.*

I reached, curling my fingers as I jerked my hands away so I wouldn't get in more trouble for touching her. I spun to put my back to her so she couldn't see my fury. I cursed. All I could do was close my eyes as I faced away from her to try to calm this beast who rattled my insides. Who the hell was this person taking over me? He wasn't obedient. Not really, but he needed to be.

"*What?* Slave, if you don't—Oh…God."

I did turn then. Charlotte's eyes were round as she headed for the mirror and continued to look down and hold her injury. The damn bruise had to have been a good five inches long. And thick, too. Fist? I didn't think so. Kick?

There was nothing I could do but stare at her and wait. Wait for a lie. An excuse. She didn't give me either as the shock melted away and was replaced by nothingness.

"Slave, get my phone from my purse."

Calm. Eerily so. She was a good actress. Turning, I obeyed. The moment she had it in her hand, I watched her transform. The strong Mistress had returned, not the scared woman I'd seen moments before.

"Main Master, this is Mistress B-Three, I'm calling in regard to your lack of security in the outside city." She got quiet. "Yeah, something *did* happen; I was attacked by one of your Masters. Master seventy-one to be exact, Norman Free. Which shouldn't surprise me since we've already had a run-in here before." Again, she got quiet. "I'll tell you exactly what it was over. The first time he saw me, he recognized who I was. He started naming movies I was in. In short, I told him I wasn't her down here, and not to pretend to know me on the outside world. I was pissed. Apparently, he was too. He kept saying something about Whitlock. About how Mistresses shouldn't be down here. He's wrong. I belong here just as much as him. What pisses me off even more was how it even happened to begin with. This was uncalled for. Everywhere else in the Gardens you have more security than Washington D.C. That attack should have never happened. If you have a facility of both genders, you better pray like fucking hell you can keep both sides safe. This incident outside was a disaster; a failure in your security protocols." Another pause. "No, I don't need to go to the hospital. I'm not dying, just beat to hell. Damn right. It was outside a place called Penski's or Pentski. I don't know. A fucking bar or something. No, I don't need you to come over. Yes, I'll send pictures. Okay."

She hung up, handing me the phone.

"Not one more outburst as I take off these pants. You have no emotion, slave. You're here to observe at the moment and take pictures, and that's it."

Was there more bruising?

"Next time—"

"No," she snapped, cutting me off. "I will not be shielded by a man just to walk down the fucking street. You're missing the point here, slave. This place has an obligation to protect the people who pay for it. Am I expecting it to be run flawlessly? No. Instances will occur. I get that, but they should be far and few between. If I don't make a stand right now, it will never change. Someone has to advocate or wolves and lions wage war.

I will not live in fear of having to watch my back, and I will not solely rely on you to take me somewhere I want to go. The Main Master will fix this, or I will bug the shit out of him until he does."

She had a point. One I should have understood before she even spoke. I didn't forget her identity, but I should have taken into account what it was outside of this place. Charlotte was big into taking a stand. She led and was the face of programs that focused on protecting those who needed it. She was strength, power. This was who she was, but it stemmed from something. As I looked at her, I was sure I knew all too well what that was.

"You're right. I'm sorry. Take off your pants. I'll get the pictures."

And I did, of all four bruises on her legs. One big baseball size one on her upper thigh. Three small quarter-sized ones under that. They were there, but not too dark yet. And they didn't seem to be affecting her too badly.

As my Mistress stood facing the mirror, texting the pictures, I reached up, unhooking her bra. Flattening my hands on her back, I rubbed up the skin, pushing the material up over her shoulders. The softness tightened underneath me, drawing up in goose-bumps. They brought my eyes up to the back of her neck that was exposed from her hair being over one shoulder. I glanced at the mirror, spinning to turn on the shower before I caused her to get even angrier.

Charlotte put the phone on the counter and faced me as I pulled back to get out of the spray. Her bra was sitting on the floor and her panties were still on. Nude lace, just like her bra had been. Their cut was arched high, accentuating her curvy hips.

"Are you going to stare or come finish undressing me?"

Heading forward, I lowered, kneeling level with the one thing I wanted more than anything. My fingers hooked in the panties, and I slowly peeled them down, soaking in the smooth folds of her pussy. Would she allow me to taste her? Touch her. Fuck her? God, I would have done anything to feel her around my cock.

"You want it so bad you can't stand it." She stepped high, removing one of her legs from the lace and then the other. She left me there, crouched, level with her ass as it swayed with her advance to the shower.

Charlotte pulled open the door, turning to throw me a look.

"I don't have all night for you to take your turn. I told you I'm tired. Get undressed and get in. You can wash me quicker that way anyway."

My shirt tore from over my head at my impatient pull. I jerked at the button of my jeans, pushing them and my briefs down. This was a first. A first of many to come? God, I could only dream.

I headed forward, opening the door and joining my Mistress. Burning slightly pulled at my neck, and I trailed my fingers over the medical-grade plastic covering me.

"The tattoo artist said it should be okay to get wet. The water won't get through. I'll look over it when we finish, just in case, and make sure everything's okay."

Nodding, I wasn't sure I could keep the anticipation off my face. For her to care for me, touch me…God, I needed it. I could touch her all day long, but it wasn't the same from her doing it of her own free will.

I stepped in as water bounced out from Charlotte's wet hair. It was so long when it was wet. Inches from her ass. It swayed at her movements, darkening to a jet black. With her eyes closed, mine ate every inch of her alive. Her breasts were full. Round. Definitely natural which was surprising with her being from Hollywood. I wasn't ever sure. Outside of bathing suit shots from paparazzi, she'd never done a movie topless. Come to think of it, she never really showed much cleavage as well. She was perfect. Gorgeous. And she was getting closer which only meant one thing: she caught me.

My gaze tore itself from her as I spun for the shampoo, pouring a generous amount in my palm. Charlotte was more out of the water waiting for me as I turned and reached up to lather the soap in her hair. Pressure around my hard cock had me squeezing my fists in the long locks. A sound left me, and I tried to concentrate enough to keep massaging the soap into her scalp.

"Mistress." Again, my fists drew in. She winced but brought her palm over the head of my cock, using my precum to lead her rolling back on my length perfectly. She tilted her head back into the stream, letting soap pour down her skin as it raced for the drain. I kept my hands in place, using them to help clear out the suds. Even when they were gone, I couldn't let go. She was stroking me fast, using both of her hands to hold me.

"Don't. Move." She lowered, looking up at me as she got to her knees and brought the tip of my cock to her mouth. The first swirl of her tongue had my toes curling in. I sucked in a breath, holding it as her lips encased the head. Sensations of all degrees sent everything from ecstasy to electrical zaps through my entire being. I held her tightly, moaning as she opened bigger and began inching me into her mouth.

"Fuck." Warmth. Suction. "Mistress, yes. Fuck."

With her hand, she stroked, moving her mouth up and down. Her tongue molded to the underside of my cock, and each withdrawal was magic all its own. Deeper she went. Faster. Just when I was about to tell her she needed to stop, she did, but only to lift my cock and began sucking on my balls. My eyes flew open, rolling through the pleasure. I almost came. I sure as fuck wanted to, but I craved to be inside her for that. I wanted her pussy. Needed the wet heat around me.

"I want to kiss you. Mistress." I was already using my grip on her hair to pull her to stand. She didn't like it, but she wasn't fighting or yelling at me either. "Mistress, I'm asking your

61

permission. I'm…begging you." Still, I drew her closer with my hold. Our lips were only an inch apart. Less?

"No."

She grabbed one of my wrists waiting until I finally let go.

My cock throbbed. Precum dripped from me in a steady stream. God, she was going to kill me and not even in the literal sense.

"Sit."

She pointed to the bench, following as I obeyed. Her leg lifted over mine, resting on the seat next to me. That was all she needed to do to have me grabbing her ass and pulling her pussy into my face. I sucked to her folds, right over her clit. Fingers held to my short hair, and I took my time tracing her slit and teasing her by pushing my tongue into her entrance.

Repeatedly, my cock jerked as she moaned through her rocking. I let go of one side of her ass, moving up her inner thigh until my finger traced a circle around her opening. I waited for some sort of sign she wanted more. When she sank down on my digit, I didn't hold back. Tightness enveloped my long length and I moved at a slow pace as I began fucking her with my finger.

"Slave." She sucked in a deep breath as I added another, stretching her even more. "Slow." I obeyed. "There. Yes."

Adding more suction over her clit, I listened as her deep sounds turned to whimpers. I let go flicking over the sensitive nerves, adding to her blissful burn as I moved in leisurely circles around the bud.

"Fuck. Slave. Slave." More intakes until Charlotte pulled back and cupped her hands over my cheeks. Her lips crushed into mine and she pushed me back to straddle my waist. With my arm I held tightly at her lower back. With my other hand, I grabbed onto my cock bringing her down on me to push into her entrance. I wasn't sure who moaned louder as I began to inch inside of her. She moved up. Down. Up. Down. I was halfway inside when she bit against my lip and sank down the rest of the way. My arms tightened as I held her still.

There was no fucking way I was going to ruin this the first time. No fucking way I'd come and make her regret going this far.

WO166

Had I thought the other slave completely ruined his chances with the Mistress? Maybe after the yelling and crying, I had secretly hoped, but that hadn't been the case at all. At least not for long. It couldn't be from what I was pretty sure was happening behind that closed door.

"Yes. God, yes."

The slapping sounds of skin pretty much told me whatever he was doing was good. How many times had the Mistress said 'more'? I tried covering my ears. It hadn't helped. She'd repeated that word more than I wanted to think about. How long had they been in there anyway? Thirty minutes? An hour? There'd probably be no hot water for me.

"Faster. Faster. Just like that."

"Ugh. Enough," I ground out, trying to turn on my other side.

But it wasn't enough for them. Minutes kept passing until both of them gasped and moaned and probably had the best orgasms of their lives. It sounded like it anyway. Me? Nope, not me. I was just an untouched virgin and would die that way. Go figure. Maybe it was for the best. What else would it be? Me, being rescued and ravaged by the insanely hot newly tattooed

God? Yeah right. He was so glued up the Mistress's ass, that would never happen. Not that I cared. I didn't want to have sex with him, or anyone. Maybe that was the only blessing I got out of this entire mess.

The water turned off, and I pulled the blanket over my head, only to rip it down. I couldn't pretend to sleep, I had to pee. I needed to shower. I wanted some food. The Mistress had come back to give me a sandwich for lunch, but she disappeared again after that. Would she forget to feed me? Maybe she just didn't want to.

Mumbled words buffered from behind the door. When it finally opened, the Mistress swept right past me. She went into the closet, returning with new clothes.

"You have half an hour to eat, shower, and do what you want. First, your blood."

Dammit. Had I thought she'd forgotten about that part. My finger squeezed into the chain that held the shackle and I held out my free arm as her pet took the knife. As he came forward, I took in the tattoo that covered from just behind his chin, all the way to his collar bones. He even had CW on his face just under and off to the side of his right eye. I'd never cared for tattoos or this look, but on him it actually appealed. It was a little scary and hadn't that been the point?

Darkness? Hands? I squinted as I took in what was clearly swirls of fog at the top. Below it, halfway down his neck were the hands of souls reaching upward towards his face. Details tattooed emerged between the ghostly bodies of what looked like tombstones in the background. They were crying out or... screaming? Scary, yes. I wasn't sure I liked it after all.

Pressure gripped my arm and pain exploded causing me to jump from the already building anxiety.

"Watch it, slave, that was deep. I'm not ready for you to kill her yet."

The Mistress bent down to look, but I didn't see her. I

couldn't even consider what she'd meant by that. The slave wasn't speaking or even listening to her. He was glaring inches from my face. More fear. Lots of it. It took me over as his warning came through clearer than if he'd spoken the words to my face. He didn't like my disregard of his Mistress's pain. He didn't like me enjoying their fighting, and now he was showing me that. But it was worse. It was acknowledgement that he knew where I stood, and it wasn't with them. This was a death threat to the core.

"I'm sorry, Mistress. It must have slipped."

"Don't let it happen again."

But the knife didn't slip. He handed over the blade, swiping my blood as he smeared it over her rosy features. Bright red streaked over her forehead, moving towards her temple. She was already glowing under the red. He'd fucked her flushed and now she wanted my blood too. They both did.

"After you're finished, get the first aid kit. That one's going to need a bandage."

"I'll take care of it. I'm sorry. I'll be careful next time."

His tone was soft and soothing despite the fact that he didn't mean it. The way he was looking at her again just increased my anger, making the fear fade. How he could feel anything for her baffled me. It was one thing if he was pretending but he wasn't. He truly adored her even though she treated him like garbage.

"Mistress, I want to eat first. What food can I have after this?"

The red darkened, half drying, half beading over the surface. "You're not allowed to cook anything. It's too late and it'll take too long. There's wraps, rolls, soup, and sandwiches. Like I said before, you have half an hour. Use it wisely because you don't get a minute more.

MISTRESS B-0003

Routines were something I needed, and surprisingly enough, me and my slaves were working out a lot better than I could have imagined. Ten days had gone by since the auction, and only once had I needed to use real punishment on either. Mark hadn't liked me putting him back in his place after I let him fuck me, but he had to see he wasn't getting in my bed until he realized it wasn't his. *Ever.* One night, fine. Two...I wasn't ready for that. But this new routine I'd slipped in and let him adopt; this I liked.

"Mistress, please."

The vibrations from his begging had me rocking faster against his face. Maybe I should have beaten him for crawling into my bed while I'd been asleep, but this was too good; I didn't want to stop. Now, every morning, he woke me up like this, and I allowed it despite I wouldn't give him sex again like he truly wanted.

"Mistress."

"Shut up or I'm kicking you out."

My head lifted as his tongue pushed into my entrance. His thumb was just above my clit, pulling back with just the perfect pressure to tip the scales on my orgasm. The need for release grew, and I cried out as he brushed his tongue over the sensitive area.

Spreading my legs wider, I almost came as his finger eased into me. This part almost got me every time. It had in the shower, but so far, I was able to restrain from his cock. How, I hadn't a clue. It was so big and thick. It was addicting, and perhaps that's why I proceeded with caution.

"Fuck, I love the way you taste."

A second finger entered causing me to grip the thick comforter. I lifted it, meeting my slave's light eyes as he stared up at me from underneath. His transformation so far was shocking. Dreamy. It was everything I wanted and that made me pull back from him even more, which didn't make sense. Hadn't this been my plan? Yes. Didn't I ruin every man I'd ever gotten close to? Also, yes. But couldn't I ruin him guilt-free? Did it really matter if I did? Wasn't he disposable? Replaceable? Hadn't that been the point and the initial appeal when I came up with the plan to get a bodyguard who would help me kill for virgin blood?

I jerked the comforter down so I wouldn't see him. I wouldn't think about any of that. It was too early to worry about what-if's anyway. Another two weeks and I'd be leaving. Time apart might be exactly what we needed. Maybe I'd see this wasn't as good as I thought. Or *he* wasn't as good? After all, he was only a man. *A slave.*

My mouth shot open as my head lifted through the suction. It'd been more powerful. Combined with the thrusts, I was losing my control. His skills blew me away. His care. His effort. Maybe one more time wouldn't hurt. Then I could drive him crazy with waiting it out again. One more time. Dammit, I was so close.

"Fine, *hurry*." I pushed under the blanket, making grabbing motions for him to come up. He didn't hesitate. My slave's lips crushed into mine and his cock entered me torturously slow. The tattooed muscles tightened on his shoulders and arms as he held himself up over me. It had my lust increasing even more as I soaked in his tattooed chest and stomach.

Mark rocked, grounding himself into me as he pushed deep. Holding his hips, I watched his thick cock become longer, only to disappear into me again. My breaths grew shallow, and I squeezed my eyes shut knowing if I continued, my orgasm would hit me within seconds.

"I want to come in you again, Mistress. I want to come so deep, you feel me inside of you all day. You can leave me here when you go out, take me, or lock me in the closet again, I'm still going to be in this pussy. I belong here." Teeth tugged against my earlobe, moving to scrape down my neck as he sucked hard. Pushing my nails into his back, I got satisfaction in his pained wince.

"You belong where I want you."

"Which is where?"

He slammed into me making my stare shoot to his. I'd almost come with no control. I was hanging on by a thread.

"Here," he moaned. "You want my cock in you because we know it's yours."

"Stop talking and just fuck me."

"Whatever you want, Mistress."

That was not the response of a slave. Not the tone, anyway. He said the right words, but he didn't mean them like he implied. Fingers pushed through my hair, tightening as I allowed him to pull my head back. His cock was already buried inside me. I arched impossibly more, feeling him not give me an inch to right myself. He kept me there, steadily thrusting with enough power to push me down into the mattress. Had I been clear-headed at all, I would have put a stop to it, but he was hitting the perfect spot. Over and over, his entire length rubbed over it until I knew I couldn't stop myself.

"Slave. W-Wait. I…Oh God. I'm not…ready. I." Spasms

shook my legs, and I tried twisting through the pleasure. Mark was pounding harder to my trapped self. So hard another orgasm rolled right over the first and it had me screaming. A loud moan rumbled from his throat, and I dug into his back with everything I had as hot cum pumped into me. By the time he was done, I was still twitching and floating in my bliss.

"Breakfast?"

He kissed my cheek as he climbed off and dropped down to the mattress next to me. I didn't give him the pleasure of making himself at home. I lifted my feet, pressing them into his stomach to push him off the bed.

"Towel, not breakfast. You can clean me and then make my food as I take a shower."

The slave's smiling face peered over the side as he propped his chin on the edge of the mattress. "Towel and then breakfast. Got it." He rose, walking nude to the bathroom. When he returned, I was already throwing his pajama pants right at his face.

"You're too smug. Why are you smiling like that?"

The covers were eased down, and he sat on the edge of the bed, spreading my legs. For seconds, all he did was stare. Reaching over, his thumb separated me. I lifted my head watching as he took in his cum seeping free. I could feel it leaving me, and I could see the pure heat in his features as he got to witness it.

"Again?" He licked his lips, swirling his thumb over the wetness, smearing himself into my pussy. Had it not been for the head that peeked up at the end of my bed, perhaps I would have been tempted. As it was, the invasion to my privacy sent me snatching the towel from my slave's hands.

"Do you need something?"

Weakling disappeared, and Mark turned to glance towards the girl I spoke to. When anger rolled through his lax features, I tried to decipher what that meant. I may have not liked her, but he didn't really have any reason to. Or…did he?

"What is it?"

He turned to face me.

"What is what?"

"You're glaring at her enough to shoot daggers."

"Well, she ruined our moment. *Again.* She did this two days ago too when she said she had to go to the bathroom. I think she's doing it intentionally."

"I am not. I do have to go to the bathroom. I've been chained up for over twelve hours. Maybe if *you* were in chains, you'd know how it felt."

"I've been in chains before. For weeks straight. You think you have it so hard?"

"*Hey.*" I cleaned myself up, glaring between the two of them. "You are not children. You do not bicker like ones. Slave, let her out, and then go start breakfast. We have a busy schedule ahead of us. Weakling, make it fast. Today, I'll leave you free while we're out. If you're good, maybe I'll leave you out more often. But if you're not here when we return, or I see you've gotten into stuff you shouldn't…I think you know what's going to happen."

A shade of color dropped from her face. Whether it was because my slave approached her or it was my words, I wasn't sure. She looked as if she feared him, and I liked that even more. If she was afraid, she wasn't ogling what wasn't hers.

"Thank you, Mistress. I'll be good. I promise."

With that, she raced to the bathroom. Mark wanted to come back to the bed, but ultimately headed for the kitchen at my look. I was just sliding my sleep shorts back on when a knock had my head whipping in the direction. I grabbed my robe, wrapping it around me as I headed for the front door. My slave was already there waiting for my approval to answer it. I held up my palm, looking through the peephole before stepping back and nodding to him. When he opened the barrier, Main Master Elec stood there in his dark suit with his hands crossed over his chest.

"Eighty-eight."

He took in my slave, moving his attention to me as he walked in. He was followed by a blond man in the standard black uniform, and two others who were oddly older than the one I knew as the High Leader. He ran the guard, but he had to be in his early-to-mid twenties where the other guards were pushing close to my age.

"Mistress." Elec clasped his hands in front of him, still eyeing up my slave, cautiously. "We're wrapping up the investigation into your accusations. The board has gone over the video evidence and are in favor of your claims. Official charges will be filed shortly. Your choice of execution is needed. If you'd like to attend, you're free to do so."

"Execution?"

The word would barely leave me.

"That's correct. The board and I have decided an assault to this magnitude on another Mistress or Master, even by another on their level, is punishable by death. It's the only way to set the example from early on. If you'll tell my High Leader, Nineteen, how you'd like Master seventy-one executed," he gestured to the younger blond, "we will be happy to take care of it for you."

"I…Well." I closed my mouth trying to push away any guilt. The son of a bitch had beaten the crap out of me while others watched or turned their backs. He knew my identity as an actress and Mistress, and he'd tried to rape me right there by the fucking street to put me in my place for being a bitch to him. Hadn't he said as much? It was humiliating having no one help me. Terrifying to think they'd do more than watch, and join in. Had I not been trained to defend myself, I might not have been so lucky. "What are my options?"

"*Can I do it?*"

We all turned to my slave as he stepped forward. Slave. Not

Mark...eighty-eight, like Elec had called him. Why had I not thought to name him that before?

"It's my fault she was attacked, Main Master. I wasn't there when she needed me. As part of being a protector, I feel I failed my Mistress. Can I handle this for her?"

Elec turned his attention to me. Whether he approved or not, I couldn't tell. His face was blank, but his thoughts were far from empty. He was iffy about my slave. Wary. Or maybe it was my relationship with him that bothered the Main Master. Was it the tattoos or my slave's need to so easily commit murder for me? I didn't know as they all stared.

"Mistress, please. Allow me to show them why they need to stay away from you. I want to do this. We both know I need to."

Nineteen met stares with Elec and the High Leader shrugged, glancing back towards me.

"If your slave wishes to hold the weapon that ends this, it's fine with me. Mistresses need to make their mark in this world. This might be the only way. It's imperative that Masters see you hold every ounce of weight they do. Even if that is through the hand of your slave. It's the only way equality will build and keep this place running in anything close to harmony."

Elec looked skeptical of the High Leader's thoughts, but ultimately nodded.

Eighty-eight kneeled at my feet, staring up, begging with his eyes.

"Mistress, please."

"Fine, but I will be standing next to you through it all. They have to know it's because of me, and they need to see if they do something like he did, it could just as easily be their life ending."

"It's decided." Elec nodded. "At the end of the main road there is a stage. Be there at five tonight. You can choose your method then, slave. If either of you don't show, we'll take care of it for you. Good day."

M0088

B ecoming a murderer was a status that had never crossed
my mind. It wasn't a position one welcomed or looked
forward to or even wanted. As me and my Mistress stood on the
stage at the end of the outside city, I knew I was going to
embrace my new role as killer like a badge of fucking pride.

On a large projector that beamed behind us cast the Master's
sins for all to see. From it starting with his hand accidentally
knocking into her as he spoke, to him reacting to something she
said as she walked by. As my Mistress shook her head and
continued, his fingers buried in her hair, ripping her off her feet.
The way her body bounced off the road at his slam was enough
to make me see red. But then he started kicking her. Charlotte
managed to scramble to her feet, but the back of his hand
connected with her cheek, and she crumbled to the ground. It
was then that I went from seeing red to black. He dragged her
out to the center of the road, pulling at her pants to try to
remove them. Only then, she stirred and started to fight in
earnest. She managed to break free, but I didn't see her round
the corner and run towards the shop like it showed on the film.
My brain had locked in on her fear, and that's where my

mindset stayed as I paced the stage, waiting for the Main Master to give the word.

As Elec eyed me, he also was explaining the rules to the crowd. Rules they apparently already knew.

"You're all going to learn very fast that things you got away with on the outside world or at Whitlock do not apply here. Money will not save you. It may get you your darkest fantasies, but if you cross a line with Masters, Mistresses, or their property, death is the only thing waiting for you. Excuses won't help. Explanations will almost surely not be enough. Let me make this clear to those who knew him; I am *not* Bram Whitlock. I will not risk this place falling because of unruly Masters, Mistresses, or even guards getting out of hand."

He continued. "This life can be simple or complicated. It's up to you. Keep to your business, have your fun, but have respect and watch what you do. If you don't…" Elec gestured behind him to the man who was restrained between two guards. "You will die."

Master seventy-one, Norman Free, was just as my Mistress described, hours earlier. He was in his fifties, balding. He was in decent shape, but he was no match for me. His shoulders jerked, and just like in the video, he had a constant mask of anger darkening his features.

The Main Master's stare came to me as he turned and headed in my direction.

"Did you choose a weapon?"

Charlotte shifted a few feet away at the Main Master's words. My head shook.

"I don't want a weapon. I'm going to kill him myself. Just like he hurt her."

"You're going to beat him to death, is that your plan?"

I tore my gaze from Master seventy-one.

"Is it forbidden?"

"No."

I glanced back to the screen, seeing the beating repeat in a never-ending loop. That fear on my Mistress, *on what was mine*...it had my muscles flexing repeatedly as I fisted my hands.

"Then I choose myself. Me. I'm the weapon."

"I believe you are."

The tone had me breaking my stare, but Elec was waving his hand, and the guards were dragging the man over. It happened so fast that my rage exploded to the forefront ready to be unleashed. The handcuffs were taken off, and I pointed right at his face.

"You did that?"

It was a question but not one I expected to be answered. It didn't stop him from tripping over his words as he went to turn to the side of the stage. When he saw guards blocking his exit, he rushed to the back, but I had him before he got far. And like his assault, I repeated them, grabbing his neck and slamming him to the wooden slats beneath us so hard, the man's mouth opened, trying to suck in air.

"Did you think you'd have her? Have what was mine?" My fist crushed into his nose with more strength than I was aware I even harbored. I hit again, and again, feeling the solid structure give way underneath the blow to his cheek. His tooth broke off under my next punch, but I didn't pause. Months of repressed fury exploded inside me. It built with each connection I made.

Arms and legs flailed while images blinded me. Images I didn't even know existed in my mind anymore. My college came into view, quickly followed by a life I barely remembered. One that didn't seem real. My mother came in a flicker of colors. Her, when I was a child, training judo with my stepdad. He'd been screaming in my face, and I was trying so hard not to cry. I saw her after I'd fallen out of our tree in high school when I attempted to rescue my cat who'd gotten stuck up there for two days. She even appeared to me the day she dropped me off at Yale. Her smile, her tears. They were there, and then gone. I saw the bar I bounced in. Fights. Laughter. I saw the men standing over my bed as I came too from whatever drug they'd slipped me at the party. Guards. Medical staff. Beating after beating. Video after video. Doctors. Bruised knees from kneeling. The training. The training. The training. I saw black silk and the way my Mistress had it fitted over her hips as she stroked my cock. Her smile. The fear. Fear. Fear…If she was afraid, what if she didn't come back? What if she didn't trust me to protect her? Alone. Here. Without her? *Never.*

Whack!

Whack!

Whack!

Whack!

I kept going, decimating crunchy flesh. Bones were breaking through the skin. My fists were bleeding, but I couldn't stop. The questions. My own fears. They mixed with his gargling as I moved to the groin area, kicking and stomping with everything I had. Touch her? Rape her? *Fuck no.* With what? Nothing. He wouldn't have anything left by the time I finished. She was mine. If anyone got the privilege to touch her, taste her, *be in her*, it was me. Only me.

A monotone hum of his pleas was barely recognizable through the mush before me. Hips caved under my force as I made sure to cover the entire area. I circled him, looking for more. Needing to prove myself without any doubt. I stood over his body, triggered as his unrecognizable face twitched. The action activated me, sending my boot to stomp his face with crushing force. Over and over, I felt the structure of his skull cave beneath my weight. Bone punctured through his swollen, broken skin, turning him even more unrecognizable as I didn't stop.

I moved to his throat. To the beginning of his chest. Blood was covering my arms and smeared over the material, soaking parts of my white shirt. I kept looking for more places to destroy.

Kept needing to find more ways to show my Mistress where I stood. On how I'd protect her to the extreme. No one would stand a chance against me. I'd care for her. Love her. I'd defend her. *Kill for her.*

A soft hand settled on my bicep causing me to slow and stop. Silence filled the city. Not even music played anymore. So many eyes were staring right at me. Again, I wiped the sweat, smearing the blood over me with every touch. I was absolutely covered in it from head to toe. Trying to breathe, I forced myself straighter, kneeling on one knee next to my Mistress as I stared down the crowd. Her hand settled over my shoulder, showing her support. They had to see. They had to know Mistress Charlotte Wyce was off limits, and if they thought otherwise, they'd have to deal with me.

This was the beginning of something I couldn't lose. If my Mistress didn't exist to be here with me, my life was literally gone. Suddenly, that didn't seem as important as keeping her happy and mine. Death was easy. Death was absolute. Not having her was unbearable to even comprehend.

"Take it in everyone because if you don't, this could very well be you. We have rules for a reason. Do not bring your outside life into this place, and think twice before asking anyone about theirs. Let's pride ourselves on privacy and respect everyone else's." Elec put his hands behind his back as he faced them again. "On another note, while I have you here, for those who bought tickets to the ball, doors open in three hours. If you signed up for the human hunt, it starts at midnight. If there's nothing else, I'm late for dinner."

He didn't even wait for questions. The man bounded down the stairs, immediately surrounded by his High Leader and four other guards holding automatic weapons. It was as if this first public death hadn't phased him in the least. Charlotte tugged me, and I let her lead me down to the surrounding apple trees below. When we were behind one of the trunks, her hand came up to wipe blood from my face. She didn't speak, but she didn't have too. Her eyes were dilated, making the blue almost black. Although she was shaky and appeared out of it, she searched my depths, trying to read me. She was worried and concerned over where I was in my head, despite that I could tell she wasn't normal in hers. I didn't speak either. I still wasn't sure I could as I took her deeper amongst the trees to hide us. Her kiss was automatic. It was rattled, but what I could only assume was grateful.

"Home." She held to me tighter, pressing her breasts into my shirt, but she wasn't letting go. Tightness hugged so firm I didn't think there was an ounce of space between us. Somehow, clarity dawned, and I eased her free, stealing one more kiss before I stood up straight. She swallowed hard, nodding as her arm linked through mine and we headed for the city. Back through the crowds that were already beginning to part for us as we walked through, and back to the one place I'd come to love and need. *Our* home.

WO166

Freedom for the slave in me was invigorating, confusing, and yet after a few hours it became calming. The silence without the chains was nice. I could feel myself lose the constant state of fear I seemed to live in. Between the Mistress I knew that wanted me dead, to the male slave who had his sights set on me, it was hard to let the fear go. Although they had different reasons, they both wanted my blood. After the days of us getting into our routine, the tables had seemed to turn. At least for my Mistress. Her anger was still there, but she'd calmed for the most part, content to have my blood for her face and not something more. It was the male slave I had to watch out for. There was something not quite right with him. Maybe it was the programming he'd undergone through the training, but when he took on the mission to protect his Mistress, he meant to do it to the death. If not his, then it would be the threat. I wasn't sure how much longer I could afford to stick around after the knife incident.

As I sipped the water by the sink, I let all the possibilities of my fate play out. My time was limited no matter what plan I concocted. Outside wasn't safe, but neither was here. I could wait out my time inside this apartment and continue my duties as the Mistress's blood slave, or I could try to escape. There had to be somewhere I could at least hide. But hadn't my Mistress been attacked while outside these walls?

I took a gulp at the frustration. When it came to size, I was lacking. Anyone out there would take one look at me, and my fate may be worse than here. They'd kill me or rape me. The stories had been endless from the guards during training. If I hadn't seen the proof of my Mistress's attack, perhaps I would have thought it was a fear tactic, but they spoke the truth. If I left here, I wasn't safe.

A low beep had me looking up. Water and glass exploded around my feet as I stared over at the opened door in horror. Blood smeared my Mistress's cheeks and around her mouth. Her big eyes were hidden behind heavy lids. Ones she kept shutting. She looked euphoric or in some sort of daze. Crimson had soaked the blouse to fit against her breasts and there were smears down her pants. I'd overheard the Main Master talk about the execution, but I had a suspicion she hadn't participated in the actual death of the man who attacked her. No. All that blood was from *him*. There was so much blood covering his entire body. Even his clothes were saturated to the point of fitting wetly against him. Light green eyes fixated right on me, and it was as if I were staring in the eyes of a rabid bear. He was still in kill mode, and he was ready to attack.

Swallowing hard, I stepped from the sink. The Mistress shut the door, but the slave hadn't moved mere feet within the barrier. He stood, staring…glaring.

"Clean it."

The Mistress's head swung to look between us. She was so out of it. His words seemed to get her attention as she gazed in my direction. I grabbed the roll of paper towels, diving to the floor.

"I'm so sorry, Mistress. You both startled me. I." I stopped as it wasn't her who came around the side, but him. Frozen, I cautiously stood, searching out the one person who I prayed would help me. Hadn't she seemed to soften to me? Hadn't she been a little nicer lately? Yes, I'd just been thinking about that.

The bloody blouse was pulled over her head and she let it fall to the floor. The slave was suddenly watching her as she began to undress and head towards the bedroom. Was she leaving me with him?

"Mistress?"

She slowed at my call, scanning over my face. The smallest tug pulled at the corner of her lips as she looked right at the male slave. She reached forward, grabbing a small remote.

"It's time. Welcome to our climax. Allow me to cue the music."

An eerie tone began to fill the space. It was a haunting instrumental with violins and other string instruments I couldn't decipher. A chill went down my spine and instinct drove me to try to sprint to the front door. A large arm wrapped around my waist while the male slave's other hand fisted in my hair. I went wild, kicking my legs and trying to rake down his face. With the way he held me, I couldn't get a good enough angle to where I could do damage.

We headed through the bedroom not even pausing as we headed for the bathroom. I screamed as I reached out, clawing and holding to the frame of the door with everything I had. For the briefest moment my hold held, but with a hard jerk I was back to clutching at air. At nothingness. And then I saw it. My Mistress was lying in the empty, over-sized, clawfoot bathtub that rested next to the shower, nude. There was no water on. She wasn't even looking at us. There was a lustful void in her eyes. She wasn't here. She was in her own internal heaven from the blood and death she'd already been a part of, and she wanted more. *She was ready for me.*

"Mistress, please. Mistress," I sobbed. "I'm a good slave.

I've been good. Please. I won't make a sound. I'll stay in the closet."

I could barely talk I was sobbing so hard. And fighting. My body felt demonic at the way I was twisting it around trying to break free. Hair tore free from my scalp, and I took the pain, content to bear it if it meant I didn't die. But she wasn't listening to me. He was though.

My eyes met his in the reflection and the slave's smirk nearly stopped my pulse.

"Please, no. Please. I'm s-sorry. I'm sorry!"

"I'm not."

"Ophelia."

My body went limp. I couldn't fight. I couldn't even speak. Not that it mattered.

The small knife he held came from nowhere. I hadn't even known he held it until I saw the reflection of him stabbing it towards my neck. Even paralyzed, my mouth somehow flew open from the excruciating pain, and I knew this was it. There was nothing left for me to do but die. I didn't even recognize the girl who was rigid now in the slave's hold as he kept the blade inside her and stared at us. Blood was beginning to pour from my wound, and the slave wanted me to see what my mistake had cost me. We turned, and colors began to blur as the sharp object ripped through my skin and I watched my blood pour down on my Mistress like her own personal faucet.

MISTRESS B-0003

L aughter. Giggling. I wasn't even sure which was coming out of me as warmth splattered against my skin. Both? God, I couldn't stop the bubbling of madness that was leaving me. No matter how many times I'd fantasized about something like this, a part of me never saw it happening. Not really. Not like this. I wasn't even sure how I'd react if it ever *did* happen. Dreaming and seeing were two different things. When I witnessed my slave crushing that man's face in, stomping it to pieces—the pure consumption overtaking him was…glorious. Fascinatingly disturbing and invigorating. He'd done that for me. He was devoted…*to me. And now this. Her.*

"Fuck, you're so beautiful when you're happy."

My slave picked up her arm, stabbing into her wrist, working the blade up towards the bend of her elbow. Where I was new to this, it was as if Mark knew exactly what to do to get the most out of making me happy. Blood ran a stream, splashing against my stomach, and when it began to slow, he shifted the corpse of the weakling, tearing the flesh open on her other arm. I stayed in that orgasmic oblivion knowing nothing but the texture of what I was covered in as he gave me my time.

Watching. Enjoying as I rubbed the blood into my face and neck.

Everything in my slave's eyes added to the experience and comfort I felt. He enjoyed this. Almost seemed to need it just as much as me. More sticky warmth gushed down as he tore his hand down the length of her chest and stomach. I laughed, rolling in the wetness as my hair swirled around my neck at the spin. I felt young again. A child who was just given everything she'd ever asked for. Mark laughed, shaking the body to empty it of what was left. More, I rubbed, even massaged the blood in, basking as I kept my lids closed. The strong smell built with every second that went by. I could even taste it through my breaths. It was taking over every part of me as I invited it through my light laughter and lick of my lips.

Footsteps brought my eyes open in time to see Mark toss the dead girl off to the side. The thud reverberated in my very soul, making me giggle even harder. I reached for him, not able to stop from pulling him down in the warm substance soaking me. His hands slid over my wet cheeks, and he met my mouth, picking me up to spin me on top of him as he slid against the bottom of the tub. It was too slippery, and he ended up on his back making him laugh just as hard as me. We were insane in our moment. Completely gone from not just rationality, but reality as a whole. All we saw was each other, covered in our coupled sins.

"Did you hear me, Mistress?" His mouth ravaged mine as fingers twisted in my dripping hair. The strong taste of iron and metallics grew, feeding me to kiss him harder.

"You're everything to me. Beautiful. Gorgeous. Stunning. Exquisite. Me and you."

"Me and you," I repeated, bringing my tongue back to duel with his, and basking in my high. I rubbed my hands down over my jaw and throat, turning to curl into my slave as more insane laughter broke through. We barely fit in the tub together, and I was more on top of him, resting on the blood of a weak slave girl, and a dead, rich, prick Master. There was satisfaction in that as well. Revenge and fantasies never tasted so sweet. I could get used to this. I could stay here forever if I wanted. With this. *With him.*

Fingers fitted over mine, leading my hand to squeeze into my breast. I was flipped on my back over him while he took his time rubbing in the blood. When he got to my lower stomach, my eyes rolled, and my legs spread to fit on the sides of the tub.

"I was made for you." He nuzzled into my neck, dipping down to rub over my slit. "We were made for each other. Next time we don't wait so long for this part."

He continued to touch me as my heart thudded like a race-horse in my chest. There were so many thoughts rolling through, but none were sticking around long enough to tempt me into deciphering them. Maybe he was right. To me, I had chosen the perfect slave. From looks to pedigree. Perhaps even his tempera-ment. He was obedient, but the part that didn't always listen was growing on me. It even turned me on with him taking me when I somehow needed it.

Minutes went by. Longer, an eternity, as the blood began to clot and dry. I lifted long enough to turn on the water. It didn't matter that he was still wearing clothes. Red splashed and swirled as the tub began to fill. Still, he touched me, teasing my nipple and rubbing over my pussy. I was so worked up, but I wasn't ready to start the night off with that just yet. I sat up, turning off the water when it was full. I barely had the strength to move. Shock. It played a big role in my behavior, but I welcomed it knowing in time it would become easier. I just had to keep going. My slave did good today, and he needed to see that.

"Mark, take this off. Tonight is special. Tonight belongs to you. But only tonight."

Light green eyes opened wide at his name. He didn't speak. Maybe he knew better as I helped him undress. Awe was etched in his features as he never once broke his attention from me. When we finally had him nude, we moved to the shower to wash out our hair. We were just as close inside, never separating more than a foot. I could tell he was exhausted but I was far from done.

"Stay undressed and climb in bed."

"Yes." He stopped, his expression growing contemplative. "Since this is special, can I call you Charlotte?"

I gave him a stern look showing him I wasn't happy, but I nodded as I wrapped the robe around me and grabbed my Mistress phone. "Only tonight. Maybe never again. And if you call me that any time but now, you will be in *so* much trouble."

"Then I'm going to say it as much as I can tonight, Charlotte."

Ringing sounded, and my slave smiled as he slapped my ass and jumped in the bed. I growled, stopping as a voice came over the other end. I randomly ordered out, but tonight we were celebrating.

"Operator."

"This is Mistress B-Three in room fourteen-twelve. I have a body pick up. I also need two steaks, sides of potatoes, some carrots, and any cake you have. Or pie. Give me both if they're available."

"Estimated pick up is eight minutes. I will put in your order."

"Great." I hung up, tossing the phone on the bed. "I'm proud of you, slave. I'm not sure what I expected when I bought you. I knew what I hoped, but I never imagined any of it would come true. I'm impressed so far. And surprised. I...I told you there would be rewards for good deeds."

"You did, not that I expect them, but I'm appreciative of anything you gift me."

"I'm glad because I'm being way too generous with you, and I'm about to get even more rewarding. Thing is, nothing's for free. You realize that? Tonight is good, but tomorrow you may hate this. It might drag on for weeks. Months. Nothing is for certain with me."

A good moment went by while he held a serious expression. "I'm here to serve you. To protect and please you. I'm yours. Whatever comes with that I'm prepared."

My heart squeezed the smallest bit with happiness, but I kept it from my face.

"Good. I will allow you to learn your esthetician stuff. I will bring in the equipment and set you up to maybe even use your skill in a main shop when I am away." Sadness, but he nodded. "We'll talk it over with the Main Master and figure it out. In the meantime, you have permission to sleep in my bed tonight. Do not get too used to that. This is the beginning of my role as a Mistress, and I'm only going to embrace it even more from here. There are rules between us, and there always will be."

I continued, taking in his seriousness. "This world and how I behave in it are nothing like what I was prepared for. Anything could happen. Maybe I'll change. Maybe I won't. What I do know is, I'm never going without this again. I've heard stories from veterans in this lifestyle, and if my future plays out like those, my need is only going to grow. Time will tell. Each Master and Mistress are nothing alike. Some are nicer than me, where others are only here to wreak havoc and slaughter at whatever cost. No one is safe. Maybe not even in their own walls. We won't think about that now. Tonight, we celebrate and focus on each other. On our beginning, together. When the time comes, we'll start planning for the next auction. I was thinking this time you could join me. Would you like to help me pick out a new slave?"

"Do I get to cum in your panties before we leave?"

Blank slate[1], my ass. Whatever had happened between us had turned my slave more man than machine, and a part of me was okay with that. He obeyed orders for the most part, and he worshiped me. *He had killed for me.*

Our smiles grew as he moved to the edge of the bed, grabbing my hips to spin me underneath him. His knee maneuvered through my thighs pushing them apart. He was already hard and ready. Once we started, I knew our night was going to be endless, just like the blood covering us had been. Just like it always would be.

"I would be *honored* to attend the next auction with you. I'm your protector. I am your *only* true slave, and I'll continue to prove it every day you let me, Mistress."

The End.

ABOUT THE AUTHOR

Alaska Angelini is a Bestselling Author of dark, twisted happily-ever-afters. She currently resides in Mississippi but moves at the drop of a dime. Check back in a few months and she's guaranteed to live somewhere new.

Obsessive, stalking, mega-alpha hero's/anti-heroes are her thing. Throw in some rope, cuffs, and a whip or two and watch the magic begin.

If you're looking to connect with her to learn more, feel free to email her at alaska_angelini@yahoo.com, or find her on Facebook.

WHEN DARK IS WHAT YOU'RE CRAVING... Step into Pitch Black with Alaska's International Bestselling pen, A. A. Dark.

OTHER TITLES FROM THIS AUTHOR

A.A Dark books
24690 (24690 series, book 1)
White Out (24690 series, book 2)
27001 (Welcome to Whitlock, 24690 series, book 2.1)
27009 (Welcome to Whitlock, 24690 series, book 2.2)
27011 (Welcome to Whitlock, 24690 series, book 2.3)
Or get all 3 novellas in the Welcome to Whitlock book below
Welcome to Whitlock (24690 series, book 3)
Black Out (24690 series, book 4)
Mad Girl (Anna Monroe series, book 1)
Never Far
MasterMind (An Anna Monroe and Never Far crossover)
Heart Lines (Anna Monroe and Boston Marks)

Alaska Angelini books
Unbearable
Insufferable
SLADE: Captive to the Dark

BLAKE: Captive to the Dark
GAIGE: Captive to the Dark
LILY: Captive to the Dark, Special Edition 1
CHASE: Captive to the Dark
JASE: Captive to the Dark
The Last Heir
Watch Me: Stalked
Rush
Dom Up: Devlin Black 1
Dom Fever: Devlin Black 2
This Dom: Devlin Black 3
Dark Paranormal/Sci-Fi lover? Check out Alaska's other reads...

Wolf (Wolf River 1)
Prey: Marko Delacroix 1
Blood Bound: Marko Delacroix 2
Lure: Marko Delacroix 3
Rule: Marko Delacroix 4
Reign: Marko Delacroix 5

Sci-Fi
Atlas Lost

ACKNOWLEDGMENTS

To my wonderful betas:
Karen Preiato
Nicole Johnson
Devon Brugh
Kayla Cramer
Morgen Frances
Monica Anne Patrie
Elizabeth Jansen
Amy Martin

Thank you so much for keeping it real with your honest feedback. As an author, I am beyond lucky to have been blessed with all of you. We've now made The Gardens our new home. Here's to many, many more stories. I love you, girls!

Dee Trejo and Nadine Flotte. We keep meeting here. I love you girls! Angels. Rocks. Lifelines. Guides. You're both everything to me.

FOOTNOTES

PROLOGUE

1. A subterranean fortress housing trafficked slaves. You can read about it in the 24690 series by A. A. Dark.
2. Virgin slave. Wears a white robe during the auction. Not capitalized to show slave status.
3. Nonvirgin slave. Wears a blue robe during the auction. Not capitalized to show slave status.
4. Docile, drugged slave. Can be W or B. Heavily trained. Good for elderly or those with disabilities. Not capitalized to show slave status.
5. Ruined, disfigure slave. Convicts fall into this category. Women or men that fall into the breeding category. Black robe during the auction. The cheapest slaves.
6. Mostly male slaves who have undergone forced indoctrination through various scientific methods. (Brainwashing, programming, training, etc.) They're programmed to be focused solely on their Mistress or Master. They are made to be obedient, loyal, and protective.
7. The Main Master from Whitlock, a subterranean fortress housing trafficked slaves. You can read about it in the 24690 series by A. A. Dark.

MISTRESS B-0003

1. Virgin slave. Wears a white robe during the auction.

M0088

1. Mostly male slaves who have undergone forced indoctrination through various scientific methods. (Brainwashing, programming, training, etc.) They're programmed to be focused solely on their Mistress or Master. They are made to be obedient, loyal, and protective.

MISTRESS B-0003

1. Mostly male slaves who have undergone forced indoctrination through various scientific methods. (Brainwashing, programming, training, etc.) They're programmed to be focused solely on their Mistress or Master. They are made to be obedient, loyal, and protective.

MISTRESS B-0003

1. Mostly male slaves who have undergone forced indoctrination through various scientific methods. (Brainwashing, programming, training, etc.) They're programmed to be focused solely on their Mistress or Master. They are made to be obedient, loyal, and protective.
    Whit

24735888R00060